DEATH ON

"The postman. But what a *peculiar* time—"

"Please—don't disturb yourself. I'll go."

And then she saw what lay on the mat. A black-haired doll dressed in poppy-strewn chiffon which she now remembered matched the blouse Suzi Barlow had worn at the lecture yesterday. But the full truth didn't dawn on her until she picked it up. The cheeks were scored with slashes of red ink and an ordinary pin had been driven through the heart . . .

Books you will enjoy
from Keyhole Crime:

DEATH ON
A BROOMSTICK

G. M. Wilson

KEYHOLE CRIME
London · Sydney

First published in Great Britain 1977 by
Robert Hale Limited

Copyright © G. M. Wilson 1977

Australian copyright 1981

Philippine copyright 1981

This edition published 1981 by
Keyhole Crime, 15-16 Brook's Mews,
London W1A 1DR

ISBN 0 263 73524 9

Made and printed in Great Britain by
Cox & Wyman Ltd., Reading

CHAPTER ONE

Miss Turnberry made exquisite dolls.

She was a kindly, anxious, gossipy bean-pole in her sixties, dressing like a genteel rag-bag and living in a cluttered flat over a butcher's shop in Wrexley High Street, but—she made exquisite dolls. Rag dolls, no more than six inches high, with painted faces, floss-silk hair and delicate, colourful dresses sewn with tiny stitches and minute embroidery, which went like a bomb at church fetes and charitable jumble-sales. Children loved them. Knowledgeable people had even begun to collect them with an eye to future antique value. The vicar's wife, for instance, proudly exhibited two neat shelves of them to interested visitors, and most Bring-and-Buy addicts were lumbered with at least one.

Miss Purdy, in the ground floor flat of her Victorian house in Church Lane, had three, sitting sedately on the bedroom mantel-shelf.

Two had been presented to her some months ago by Miss Turnberry herself, copies of Dresden-china shepherdesses, quite pretty but of no particular interest. The third was different. With its long black hair and pert expression it reminded her irresistibly of her top-floor tenant, and seeing it on the crafts-stall the day after she'd agreed to let the flat to Shirley and her prospective husband, she'd bought it as a good omen. Shirley herself couldn't see the likeness and had taken a queer aversion to it, but as she rarely entered the ground floor flat and never the bedroom, Miss Purdy didn't allow this to interfere with her own harmless

7

pleasure. She'd given it the place of honour in the middle with a demure shepherdess on each side, all three sitting prettily against the rose-patterned wallpaper eyeing the bedroom with passive approval.

So why was it only the six-inch Shirley she found lying prone on the tiled hearth after a quick visit to the super-market one April afternoon?

In the act of taking off her hat she stopped and looked down at it, mystified. What had caused it to fall? The rattle of passing traffic? But there was rarely much traffic in this quiet by-lane opposite the church and *never* heavy lorries. Movement from above? The intermediate floor was occupied by Mrs. Sibley, a stout heavy-treading widow in her fifties, but the heaviest of treads could hardly have shaken down one of three almost identical objects and left the others undisturbed. An intruder? But all doors were locked and all windows tight and nothing else was out of place. There seemed no rhyme or reason to it.

Fortunately no harm was done. Miss Purdy picked it up, shook off non-existent dust, spent a moment admiring the neat little leather boots for the twentieth time and set it back in its place, writing off the incident as peculiar but not nearly so important as a cup of tea. She went out to the kitchen to put the kettle on.

*   *   *

After tea she found herself thinking of the real Shirley Carter rather than the mimic one. She liked both Shirley and her new, gawky young husband, but there was no doubt the girl was inclined to be—well, fanciful. Which wouldn't have mattered if she'd kept her fancies in the family, so to speak, but now she'd drawn in Mrs. Sibley—

Miss Purdy frowned. She definitely didn't like Mrs. Sibley. The latter had been in the house six weeks, the

8

young Carters less than three, and already the trials of being a landlady were beginning to show. And she had only herself to blame. Three months ago, when her former landlady had put the three-storeyed house up for sale and she'd proposed buying it, her forthright friend Inspector Lovick had warned her what she was letting herself in for.

"Rent Acts and tribunals and heaven knows what, it's a mug's game these days and you're still shaky after two doses of hospital. Take my advice, keep your money in the bank and let some other mugs have the headaches. They can't turn you out."

"It isn't as simple as that. For one thing, I'd have no control over who lives upstairs, and for another I'm thinking of my work. The new book barely half-finished—"

"They can't stop you typing."

"I haven't typed a word for weeks. The truth is, Inspector, I'm getting old and—my mind—isn't as active as it was."

First time in the twenty-odd years he'd known her she'd ever admitted to weakness. . . . Looking closely at her drawn, pale features, he'd realised the last affair—triple murder which had nearly claimed her as a fourth victim—had taken more out of her than he'd suspected.*

His voice had roughened with genuine anxiety. "All the more reason—"

"Please—let me finish. If I invest my savings in the house and let the two upstairs flats to nice people, it will give me an income and allow me to take things easy for a while, finishing the book at leisure."

"And suppose they aren't nice people?"

"I won't take them without references, I promise you."

"And a fat lot of good that'll be if—oh, I give up!" He'd flung up his hands in a characteristic gesture, disclaiming all further responsibility. You can't order a woman

* SHE SEES THINGS.

of fifty-odd about as if she were a child, or spank sense into her either, however much she deserved it. Whatever he said she wouldn't take a blind bit of notice, so he might as well save his breath. " But don't blame me when you find you've bought trouble," had been his parting shot.

Which I have, she thought now, staring out of her big bay window at the budding elms in the churchyard across the way, their baby-green leaves glowing golden against the dying rays of the sun. He was right and I was wrong. References are no guarantee of compatibility. . . .

Mrs. Sibley's references, for instance, had been un-impeachable, backed up by Miss Purdy's own lawyer and a local bank-manager, but the woman herself had aroused immediate antagonism by arriving on the doorstep un-announced and stating baldly : " I've come about the flat."

" The flat?" Miss Purdy had been startled as well as repelled. " But I haven't decided—I'm not sure—how did you come to hear about it?"

" Your solicitor's a friend of mine."

" Mr. Begbie? It's true he handles my affairs but he had no authority to—"

" Well, I'm here now, so where's the harm in seeing it?"

Since she was already thrusting past into the hall, Miss Purdy hadn't much choice in the matter, but she was angry with Mr. Begbie for exceeding his brief and quite deter-mined that nothing would induce her to accept such a coarse, aggressive, uncivil woman as her first tenant, how-ever good her credentials.

Unluckily it was one of the bad days to which she'd become accustomed since leaving hospital. Waking up with a raging headache, she'd had nothing for breakfast but a cup of coffee and three aspirins, swallowed ten minutes before and just beginning to take effect. As she reluctantly led the way upstairs, the anger melted into muzziness, settling into a dull, almost hypnotic lethargy during the

10

tour of the flat. In retrospect the whole episode still seemed slightly unreal, and she couldn't decide whether the aspirins, the headache or some peculiarly potent quality in the woman herself had been responsible for changing her decision. Certainly she'd never have yielded if her faculties had been working normally. The sort of tenant she'd visualised was a slim quiet middle-aged spinster like herself. Mrs. Sibley's age-group fitted, but Lovick's direst forebodings couldn't have embraced a stout, overdressed, over-scented, slightly vulgar widow with greasy-looking black hair, boot-button eyes and an unswerving determination to get her own way; one, moreover, who claimed friendship with Miss Turnberry as well as the solicitor.

She'd stated flatly: " You've got two of her dolls." (This was in the shepherdesses-only period.)

Miss Purdy had been momentarily jerked out of her muzziness. " How do you know that?"

" She told me."

" Oh."

This simple explanation might have been reassuring if Mrs. Sibley hadn't followed it up with another flat statement. " The third will bring death."

*   *   *

Lovick's reaction after his first glimpse of Mrs. Sibley lumbering upstairs had been predictable. " What in the name of wonder made you saddle yourself with that fat old fraud?"

" Why do you call her a fraud?"

" Because I've got a nose for 'em, that's why, and I wouldn't trust that one a flaming centimetre. Reminds me of a so-called medium I nicked a few years back, four legs and three arms and a toy trumpet up her sleeve, also a pair of clappers strapped to her knees which—"

11

" What do you mean, four legs and three arms?"

" Couple of false legs under the table to keep the mugs quiet and an extra arm in full view while the real one was producing flowers and whatnot out of the air and waving 'em about. Did jolly well out of it, too, I'm surprised she hadn't cleared out of the country for tax purposes—that's if she ever paid any tax. How did this one make her money —in a fairground?"

" On the contrary, her late husband owned a string of hardware shops in the Midlands and left her very comfortably off."

" Says who?"

" Her bank manager and my solicitor. They both produced unexceptionable references."

" That still doesn't explain a yen for her company." He eyed Miss Purdy's neat figure and smooth grey hair, mentally contrasting her with the unwieldy, flat-footed specimen he'd just seen waddling upstairs. Dammit, he could still smell the woman's gardenia or what-have-you, probaby cost the earth but he couldn't stand scent before lunch, it put him off his beer, besides offending his sense of rightness in this quiet house. Something at the back of Miss Purdy's eyes, however—a look of strain, worry, unhappiness, indecision—made him drop his aggressive mood and say abruptly : " Come on, out with it. Why *did* you take her?"

Miss Purdy said with complete honesty : " I don't know."

" You don't *know*?"

She said slowly : " I doubt if I can explain it to you. I'd quite determined to send her packing but—well, I had a headache, I'd just taken some aspirins and—"

" For Pete's sake! Aspirins! If you'd said LSD—"

" I don't mean I wasn't aware of what I was doing, but my resistance collapsed. She has a very strong personality

12

and—and I'm inclined to think she—she *willed* me into—"

" What utter bosh!" he exploded. " If you mean she exerted undue influence to make you sign the contract—"

" Not that exactly, but she brushed aside all objections and made my prejudices seem silly, and after I'd rung up her bank-manager and had a word with Mr. Begbie there seemed no real reason to refuse her. She insisted on my ringing up Miss Turnberry as well, and—"

" Miss Turnberry's a pain in the neck."

" She's very good-natured—"

" And very silly. I wouldn't take a cat into my house on her say-so. Old Begbie's all right, I suppose, but if only you'd consulted me first—"

" I gave her my word—or so she said—and I couldn't back out after that. She's already contacted Dillinger, the builder, and is having the whole flat redecorated. Please, Inspector—" her breath caught—" don't tell me again I've been a fool, I'm too liable to believe you. Not that she's been any trouble so far—I've hardly spoken to her since she moved in—but—I don't like her, I think I'm a little afraid of her, and—and I wish to heaven I'd been more strong-minded." The last words came out in a rush.

*   *   *

The Carters' case was simpler in one way and more complicated in another.

Heating had always been a problem in the top flat and Miss Purdy had decided to install a self-contained central-heating system before letting it. Dillinger's quotation, how-ever, was beyond her purse and although he was already in the house supervising Mrs. Sibley's redecorating, she'd decided to accept his ex-partner's more reasonable estimate instead. The trouble with this was that Dillinger and Breck had split company a few months previously and were no longer on speaking terms, and simple tact dictated that one firm should be out of the house before the other man moved in.

Miss Purdy didn't mind waiting. After her experience with Mrs. Sibley she was in no hurry to consider further tenants. It was the vicar who precipitated matters. Spotting Dillinger's truck outside he lost no time in pleading the cause of the choir's most promising young tenor.

" David Carter—you know him, of course. Fine voice and good character. Engaged to a girl in the post-office, Shirley Smith. Not one of our regulars, I'm afraid, though no doubt after the wedding—"

" When will that be?" she'd asked politely.

" As soon as they can find somewhere to live. So if by a happy chance your top flat is available—"

" Not for some weeks, I'm afraid."

She'd explained the difficulty. He'd pursed his lips. " I see your point, of course, though with Harvey Dillinger already in the house and having such an excellent reputation—however, I agree his prices—but against that one has to set—" He'd paused, looking genuinely distressed. " Oh dear! I do dislike speaking ill of—however, there's no doubt Bill Breck—you've heard of that sad affair on the housing estate? A half-built wall collapsing—a miracle nobody was hurt—really, such shoddy workmanship—"

" There's another side to that tale, Vicar. I've heard talk of vandalism. At any rate his prices are reasonable and I'm prepared to give him a chance, but it will be at least a month before I can think of letting."

But this, the vicar had declared with enthusiasm, was admirable! Precisely the right length of time to arrange the ceremony and take a short honeymoon! Knowing when she was beaten, Miss Purdy had sighed and accepted her fate, but this time with her eyes open and no regrets. She

14

liked the young couple, whose gratitude and delight after seeing the flat had rocketed sky-high, and for a full two minutes after their departure she'd basked in the warm glow of satisfaction that comes from doing a good turn to nice people.

And then Mrs. Sibley had descended the stairs. . . .

"Miss Purdy!" Her voice was at its harshest and most arrogant. "I have a stepson!"

"Really?" What else could you say to an abrupt, challenging statement like that?

"In Norwich. Married. A writer like yourself. Your top flat will suit them very well."

Miss Purdy took a moment to pull herself together. Anything more than a passing contact with her formidable tenant and her will-power seemed to slip. But this time, thank heaven, compliance was out of her power. With careful self-control, she explained that the top flat was already let.

The woman's eyes seemed to burn into her. "To those kids who've just gone out? A couple of ninnies without two ha'pennies to rub together? You must be out of your mind."

"Really, Mrs. Sibley—"

"I don't know what they're paying, but I'll top it by a couple of quid."

"It's not a question of money. I've given my word."

"Five quid."

"No."

For a few seconds the clash of wills had been almost audible. In fact, it *was* audible if you counted Mrs. Sibley's heavy breathing. And then, unbelievably, she'd turned without a word and clumped upstairs again, leaving victory with Miss Purdy but leaving something else behind as well—the knowledge that she'd made an implacable enemy for life.

Or was that impossibly melodramatic?

In a mood of slightly reckless reaction, she'd bought Miss Turnberry's 'Shirley' the next day, finding obscure pleasure in installing one of the 'kids' straight away. The mood hadn't lasted, of course; a ludicrous idea, anyway; but she'd still been able to admire the doll's delicate workmanship and take pleasure in possessing it. Not until the real Shirley's wedding-day had she remembered Mrs. Sibley's warning: "The third will bring death. . . ."

* * *

Yet there'd been no immediate repercussions from that clash of wills. During the following days Mrs. Sibley had been careful to keep out of her way. Harvey Dillinger's men had finished redecorating and departed, and Bill Breck (who couldn't afford a regular staff) had started on the heating-installation himself. After a white wedding, Shirley and David had driven off to a Clacton honeymoon, and life in the rest of Wrexley had flowed on normally. Daffodils had come out. Buds were showing hopeful signs of growth on the churchyard elms. Pussy-willows admired their own reflections in the wind-ruffled waters of Wrexley Broad. What was the malice of one ill-natured woman set against the countless blessings of a dawning Spring?

But life hadn't been all daffodils and pussy-willows. Breck's timetable had been irritatingly bedevilled by factory delays and unexpected snags in adapting stubborn Victorian innards to modern electric cables, with the result that the Carters had had to move in before the job was finished. And then—

And then Shirley had begun having fancies.

At first the 'smell' she'd complained of had been a joke to everybody but Bill Breck, who having just got all the bedroom floorboards nicely down had been obliged to take them up again to look for non-existent dead rats.

After a conscientious search he'd confessed himself flummoxed. " Naught to account for it, far as I can see. Tell you the truth, ma'am, I'm beginning to think there's a hoodoo on the place. Or on me," he'd added with intense bitterness.

" What does that mean?" Miss Purdy had asked sharply, thinking of the collapse of the council-estate wall.

" Just what I say, ma'am. Ever since me and Dillinger split up, naught's gone right for me or mine. Bad debts, missus ailing, jobs messing themselves up—"

" Are you saying there's a connection?"

" Sounds daft, don't it? But a man can't be unlucky *all* the time. Not unless he's been bespoke."

Bespoke. A queer archaic word meaning bewitched. And I'd like to have seen the Housing Officer's face if he produced that as an excuse for the wall falling down, she'd thought with a flash of humour. But her sympathy for him was rapidly diminishing. In her book, if a man was unlucky all the time it usually meant he wasn't putting his heart into the job.

Still, that didn't explain the smell.

Twice after he'd packed up his tools and departed, Shirley had suffered—or said she'd suffered—a wave of it, and then it hadn't been funny any more, either after it had caught her alone in the house in broad daylight or when she'd come home to it after shopping. She'd also claimed the new heating-system wasn't working properly, the bedroom sometimes being deathly cold even with the power turned full on, and that wasn't funny either, though there'd been no suggestion that anything but Breck's bad workmanship or carelessness was to blame.

Until Mrs. Sibley had suggested spooks.

* * *

17

The climax came when the Carters had been in the flat for just on three weeks. Arriving home tired but pleasantly relaxed after an evening with the Lovicks, Miss Purdy drank her usual cup of Horlicks, turned out the fire in the living-room, locked the door into the hall and went through to her bedroom to undress. Nothing unusual at all—except that the two shepherdesses were again sitting sedately on the narrow Victorian mantel-shelf eyeing the bedroom with passive approval while the ' Shirley ' doll lay prone on the hearth below, not looking at anything.

It was a long time before Miss Purdy was able to sleep. She'd replaced the doll on the shelf behind a large glass paper-weight so that whatever future shaking it received from causes known or unknown, it could only fall harmlessly sideways—unless it had learnt how to clear a full three inches of slippery glass before taking off.

But she was deeply worried. By now she was convinced that with Mrs. Sibley she'd let something evil into her house. Not necessarily supernatural—she wasn't convinced that either the death-prophecy in connection with the third doll, or the woman's malicious attempt to brainwash Shirley into thinking the top flat haunted, was anything more than simple intimidation—but the mind behind both things was surely malevolent and harmful. An obvious explanation of the smells and heating-troubles upstairs (if you ruled out Breck's supposed incompetence) was that Mrs. Sibley was somehow contriving them in order to frighten the couple out of the flat and secure it for her stepson and his wife. Somehow—but how? And how could her contrivances extend to pushing a single object off a ledge in a room she'd never even entered? Miss Purdy's brain turned giddy in the attempt to solve that last problem. Invention was her trade, but in this instance it failed her. There was simply no way—no way at all—no way—

18

At which point she fell asleep.

Half an hour later she was awakened by the sound of feet flying downstairs. As if jerked by a string, she sat up and switched on her bedside lamp. Half-past two. What in the name of—

That banging—shouting—

" Miss Purdy! Miss Purdy! Let me in! Quick—quick—"

" All right, Shirley! I'm coming!"

She scrambled into her dressing-gown and unlocked the hall door.

The girl almost fell into her arms. " It's happened again! I told you so! I told you and you wouldn't believe me. That *hellish* smell—" Her voice went up and up.

" Shirley, for Pete's sake!" Still tying his dressing-gown cord, David Carter stumbled into the room, rumple-haired and harassed. " Waking the house at this time of night—"

" What do you expect me to do? Turn over and go to sleep again as though nothing had happened?"

" Nothing *has* happened. Except—"

" Except Mrs. Sibley's right, there's a ghost in the place."

" Ghost my—" He broke off in exasperation. " All right, all right, I'll admit there's a nasty smell, but—"

" B-brimstone."

" How the heck does she know what brimstone smells like?"

" And so c-cold . . ." The girl was indeed shivering violently—not surprising, since all she wore was a flimsy nightdress. " That d-damned radiator—Breck ought to be p-prosecuted, he's not fit to—to—"

" Rubbish!" broke in Miss Purdy decisively. " We've had the floorboards up, he can't do more, and as for Mrs. Sibley—"

" She says the flat's haunted."

" You can't have it both ways. If it's haunted you can't

19

blame Breck. Anyhow, she knows nothing about the house, she's as much a stranger here as you are, she was simply trying to frighten you."

"Then she's jolly well succeeded. I wouldn't go up there again if you paid me. If she wants the flat she can damned well have it."

"Here, just a minute!" her husband protested. "Where are we going to find another place?"

"I'd rather live in a slum than—"

"Well, I wouldn't, and I'm ruddy well not going to move in with your mother either, it's plain daft when we've got a perfectly good—"

"It's not good, it's foul and—"

"There must be some reason for the smell. Drains—a dead rat under the—" Catching Miss Purdy's clear grey gaze he bit the sentence short. "Okay, nothing under the floorboards. I'm sorry as hell about all this, Miss Purdy. I know you've done all you can, but—"

"That's right, take her part," flamed Shirley. "Say I'm imagining it, that's what you both think, isn't it? But I'm not, I'm *not*, and it's her fault anyway, she should have warned us before we *took* the—"

"Stop!" commanded Miss Purdy, stung out of all patience. "We'll settle this matter once and for all."

Pushing the girl into a chair, she ordered David to put the kettle on and fetch the eiderdown from her own bed. Stooping, she switched on both bars of the electric fire, thankful for the silence overhead which meant (she hoped) that Mrs. Sibley was sound asleep. Leaving David to tuck the eiderdown round his shivering wife, she made tea and brought the tray in from the kitchen, pouring out a cup for Shirley that was strong and hot with plenty of sugar.

"And now, David, if you'll come up to the flat with me—"

"No!" With a wail of protest Shirley grabbed his sleeve.

20

"Don't leave me, David! I'm scared!"

"*My* flat isn't haunted," said Miss Purdy with under-standable tartness. "And I need a witness."

David stood up. "Of course, Miss Purdy. Won't take a couple of minutes, Shirley darling. You'll be all right down here."

On the way upstairs she soon became conscious of a nauseous smell polluting the air, weak at first but over-powering when they reached the top landing.

David mopped his brow. "Gosh! Talk about devilish—"

One thing was certain, it took more than a dead rat under the floor to produce such a stench.

Turning towards the bedroom—a bright, pretty room with white walls and furniture and colourful curtains—she stopped dead on the threshold. It was still a bright, pretty room if you discounted the charnel-house smell and the chill of an unseasonably cold April night in a flat with no central heating, but this flat did have central heating and the radiator was full on. . . .

It took a conscious effort of will-power to cross the room and jerk the curtains aside. She opened the casements wide to moonlight and a scattering of late frost, and drawing deep breaths of the cleansing air she found her stomach settling and her courage hardening.

After a few moments she turned back to face him. "What about the other rooms?"

"I don't know. Shirley rushed down and I—well, just followed."

"Let's go and see."

Leaving the window open, she crossed the small landing and switched on the living-room light. The smell had per-meated the whole flat to some degree but its obvious focus was the bedroom. Nevertheless she opened every window to its fullest extent in spite of David's shivering protests.

"I say, do we have to—"

" You prefer the smell?"

" Of course not, but—"

" Then we'll get rid of it."

He said with sudden violence: " That damned builder of yours—"

" I'll speak to him again."

" What am I going to say to Shirley?"

" You can both finish the night in my living-room. To-morrow—I hope—we'll be able to discuss the thing more calmly."

CHAPTER TWO

In the morning two notes were waiting for her, one on the breakfast table and the other pushed under her door. The first was from David, saying Shirley had gone home to Mum and he'd had to leave for work but they'd be back later to talk things over. The second came from upstairs. It said: 'You needn't think I didn't hear that disgraceful noise in the middle of the night for I did and it's rattled my nerves to pieces, I've a right to peace and quiet paying through the nose like I do and I'm off to ask my friend Mr. Begbie's advice so don't be surprised if something comes of it. Yours truly, S. Sibley.'

" Well!" said Miss Purdy inadequately.

Lifting the phone, she caught Lovick just as he was starting breakfast. His mind was more on soggy eggs and congealing bacon than other people's problems, and as soon as he'd grasped she was ringing up about smells he hit the roof.

" What in ruddy heck made you take the woman in the first place? Smells!" For a moment words failed him, but he rallied strongly. "What do you expect *me* to do about 'em? If you *will* employ second-rate odd-job men—"

" Mr. Breck is a qualified builder and electrician."

" You'd never guess it to hear—" He cut that short, remembering phones have ears. "Never mind, we'll talk about it later. I'll drop in some time or other—tomorrow maybe—don't wait in for me—"

" I won't," she promised acidly, and rang off, uncertain

23

at that moment which of the two she had less time for, Mrs. Sibley or Inspector Lovick. 'Some time or other', indeed! If that was all his friendship was worth—

It wasn't, of course. In times of real trouble—what *he* considered real trouble—there was no-one she'd rather depend on. The difficulty was to make him take her seriously.

Considerably put out, she drove into Norwich after breakfast and spent the day shopping, winding up with a good dinner paid for out of Mrs. Sibley's rent-money. It was past nine when she arrived home, tired and in no mood to pick up where she'd left off, but David was hovering uncertainly in the hall and she had no option but to take him into her flat. There was no sign of Shirley or—thank heaven—Mrs. Sibley.

"How is Shirley?" she asked, dropping her purchases on a chair.

"So-so. Still at her mother's. I'm sorry, Miss Purdy, but she says she's not coming back."

"So you're here to give notice?"

"Yes. I've arranged to have our stuff moved out the day after tomorrow."

"I hope you won't regret it."

"I regret it *now*," he exploded with uncharacteristic violence. "I think she's being a fool. As for that woman upstairs, I'd like to wring her neck. Her and her damned spooks—"

"That's enough!" said Miss Purdy sharply. "She's my problem now, not yours. We'll leave it at that, if you please."

She slept heavily, waking to bright sunshine which brought a more optimistic mood. Over breakfast she considered plans for the day. Mrs. Sibley? There'd have to be a confrontation sooner or later but it wouldn't hurt to let things simmer for a bit. Breck? She must insist on another inspection of his work but it could wait until the flat was empty. Meanwhile, since she hadn't the slightest intention of awaiting Lovick's convenience, she decided to go for a walk.

In the old days one of her favourite objectives had been Witchwater, a small secluded broad difficult to reach except by boat but well worth the alternative exercise, a bus-ride to the village of Felling and a long trek over the marshes. Could she get so far in her present state of health? No harm in trying. Taking a stout stick for support, she sallied forth with a heady sense of playing truant.

The bus deposited her outside Felling's only pub. From there a half-mile of rutted track brought her to Pizey's, a picturesque old cottage which had once belonged to a friend but had long been given over to strangers. From here one turned off on to the marshes proper, a seemingly limitless expanse of flat tussocky grassland criss-crossed by narrow drainage-dykes, the only landmark being a tall clump of alders nearly two miles distant which masked the approach to Witchwater.

The alders looked further away than she remembered and she halted by the stile to consider. She was by no means tired yet, but she'd have to come back as well as get there. Not directly, though; the northern bank of Witchwater (where once a cottage had stood) was carpeted with lush green grass where she'd be able to take a good rest. I'll risk it, she decided. I'm not quite decrepit yet. . . .

Clambering over the stile, she set off with a good heart. The ground was drying nicely after the winter's damp but it wasn't yet hard enough for cattle, and her foot occasionally went down into a treacherous pocket of mud or squelched through standing water. Still, these were minor hazards to set against the spreading beauty of marsh-marigolds, and nobody could deny the company of meadow pipits and yellow wagtails was infinitely preferable to that of Mrs. Sibley. Crossing the first dyke by its rickety plank

25

bridge, she felt better than she'd done for months.

By the time she reached the path through the alder-copse, however, she was feeling the need not only for that rest she'd promised herself, but for a cup of tea or coffee. Why hadn't she thought of bringing a Thermos? No chance of refreshment at Witchwater, she reflected wryly. Now if only the Daws' cottage hadn't been burnt down—

It was the Daws who had given the broad its name. For generations a reputation for witchcraft had clung to them, culminating in the sixteen-hundreds when one of them had been burnt at the stake and the original hovel destroyed. A sturdier cottage had replaced it, lasting till Jessica Daw, a teen-ager and the last of the line, had been murdered there a few years ago and the murderer had sent it up in flames to conceal her body. Locals had always given the place a wide berth and even now, with the cottage reduced to weed-grown rubble, the site was generally shunned as unholy. All to the good in one way, since the infrequent visitor was assured of solitude and peace, but there are occasions in life when even an ice-cream van or roadside café has its beauties, and just now Miss Purdy would have settled for anything with a kettle and tea-pot. . . . At which point she emerged from the trees and came to a blank stop.

Witchcraft—or magic? Hallucination—or mirage? On the grassy bank where the Daw cottage had stood for centuries it was still standing—in spite of having been burnt to the ground. She saw it as clearly as if—as if—

As if it were real.

For a few moments the world seemed to spin and she was obliged to grope for support towards the nearest tree-trunk. Then, as her brain cleared, she looked again, fully expecting to see nothing but willow-fringed water, emerald grass and old rubble choked with dead weeds. But the cottage was still there—lath-and-plaster walls, latticed

26

windows, reed-thatched roof and all.

She drew a long shaky breath, her emotions curiously mixed. On the credit side she wasn't crazy or the victim of enchantment and she hadn't taken a supernatural step back into the past. The building looked real because it *was* real; somebody had cleared the site and built a replica. On the debit side, she had the strongest possible conviction that rebuilding shouldn't have been allowed. Old evils had been resurrected as well as walls and roof and windows. On a site so saturated with malice and hatred and wickedness, it was dangerous lunacy to introduce new life.

That apart, she had to admit the job had been superbly done. As far as she could recall from photographs (she'd never seen the original) it was an exact copy, using genuine old timbers, blending into its setting as perfectly as its predecessor.

So why was she so repelled by it? It wasn't as though she'd known the dead girl. The murder had taken place before she'd settled in Norfolk and all she knew about it came from Lovick, who never referred to it without a snarl of distaste.

" Damned young fool," was his favourite version. " The girl, I mean. No more a witch than my left foot. A dollybird for looks, if that's any recommendation, but once she got hold of that cat—"

" What cat?"

" Stray she picked up from the marshes. Black as sin and savage as a tiger. Personally I'd sooner have given bed and breakfast to the tiger. Way he went for me on sight—" He rubbed his leg reminiscently. " Can't wonder the folk round here started talking of familiars, especially as she could do anything she liked with the brute. Made my skin crawl to see him rub up against her, purring like some blasted kitten. And a silver collar round his neck, I ask you! That's what put the villagers against her. Supposed to be the original familiar's collar from way back when the first Daw copped it—mentioned in local history somewhere—and young Jessica played it for all she was worth. Said she'd found it in the attic but it's my belief the silly young fool bought it from some junk-shop and used it to put the fear of hell into anyone who crossed her. Elimauzer, she called him. Finding herself the last of the Daws went to her silly head."

" What happened to the cat after she—"

" Shot," said Lovick laconically.

" And the silver collar?"

" Back to some junk-shop, I suppose. Not the sort of memento I'd care to have around myself."

Not that it mattered, of course. Only curiosity had made her ask. With no more Daws left to claim it—

She stiffened suddenly. Someone was watching her, she felt sure of it. Turning her head swiftly, she found she was right. From the roof of a brand-new boathouse a huge crouching black cat was eyeing her with baleful hostility. And the cat wore a silver collar . . .

* * *

' Pretty pussy ' hardly seemed the right approach.

She liked cats as a rule but this one, appearing so pat on her recollections, was quite a different matter. She might even have turned and run if there'd been anywhere but the cottage to run to, and if she hadn't known in her bones he'd be after her with claws out the moment she turned her back. She'd never before seen a cat with quite that look of malignance.

She flicked a quick glance at the cottage. So far there'd been no sign of human movement but smoke was rising from the chimney and there was a good chance someone was at home. If she could be sure they'd take her side and

28

not the cat's—

The cat moved first. But not in her direction, thank heaven. His whiskers twitched and his swivelling eyes gave warning of someone's approach round the side of the cottage. Seconds before the young woman appeared he leapt down and streaked across the grass towards her— or rather towards the basin she was carrying.

Miss Purdy sighed with relief. Silver collar or no silver collar, there's nothing hobgoblinish about a domestic pet wanting his dinner.

The surprise was in the girl's reaction. Taking a quick step back she held the basin high out of his reach, her voice shrill with panic. " Get away! Nothing here for you! It's only—oh, you—you *devil*!" She gasped with pain as an impatient claw sank in her leg. " You vicious brute! One of these days I'll—I'll make Ken shoot you, I don't care *what* they say."

Dropping the basin, she pulled up the left leg of her slacks and dabbed distractedly at a long red weal. The cat, finding the basin empty, lost interest and stalked off towards the back of the building, entirely disregarding the threats being screamed after him.

Miss Purdy stepped forward and said with cordiality : " I quite agree."

" Oh!" The girl jerked round with her mouth open. " I'm sorry, I didn't realise—"

" For heaven's sake don't apologise! I'd like to thank you. If you hadn't diverted him I think he'd have attacked me."

" So I got it instead. Damn the brute! Not that I think he meant—oh well." She gave the scratch a final dab and dropped the trouser-leg. " It was the basin, of course, and all I wanted was eggs. The chickens lay all over the place and—" She broke off, looking at the newcomer closely. " Miss Purdy, isn't it?"

" Yes, but I'm afraid—" Miss Purdy stopped in her turn. From the beginning she'd fancied the girl's features were familiar but hadn't been able to pin a name to them. Long fair hair, ingenuous blue eyes, small face with the sheen of youth—memorable enough, one would think, but between memory and reality lay a difference, something teasingly off-key. And then she had it. Last time she'd seen this face it had worn a gloss of sophistication—elaborate make-up and false eyelashes—and a smart office frock had preceded shabby red pullover and faded jeans. Take away the fancy stuff and you almost had a different person. But where—

" Mr. Begbie," said the girl helpfully. " I was his secretary."

" Of course! And your name is—wait a minute—Marjorie—"

" With a G, not a J."

" Margery Martin," produced Miss Purdy with triumph. " Right?"

" Wrong." The young eyes danced with laughter. " I was married on New Year's Day."

" Were you, indeed! I wish I'd known, I'd have sent my congratulations. And what's your name now, my dear?"

Margery gave a little giggle. " You'll never believe it, it sounds so silly, like being Mrs. Humpty-Dumpty or Polly Flinders, straight out of Mother Goose."

" What *do* you mean?"

" Can't you guess? Think of see-saws."

" See-saws? But—" She checked abruptly. It wasn't possible. This cottage—the black cat—that silver collar—Witchwater—

" I'm Margery Daw," said the girl obligingly.

*　　*　　*

30

Tea was forthcoming after all, and whatever disquieting thoughts were churning around in Miss Purdy's mind after Margery's disclosure that Daws were still extant, at least she was able to consider them in comfort beside a pleasant fire.

She looked around the living-room with curiosity, noting the old-fashioned range, flagged floor and a narrow flight of stairs leading upwards behind a half-open door in the far corner. A primitive kind of lay-out but not unattractive. Half-apologetically, Margery explained that it was an exact reproduction of its predecessor. " You know, the cottage that got burnt down a few years back. Done it very nicely, haven't they? Bit on the small side but we don't mind that, though when the baby comes—I'm three months gone, you know—"

" Congratulations again."

" I don't know what'll happen then. I mean—just this one room downstairs and the kitchen out there, and two small beds above—no bathroom even—I jibbed a bit at that but Mr. Dillinger said it 'ud be completely out of period."

" Harvey Dillinger, the builder?"

" You know him?"

" He's been working at my house quite recently. Not for me but for my tenant, Mrs. Sibley."

" Mrs. Sibley! That old—" Margery pulled an expressive face. " But I'd better not say anything if she's a friend of yours, had I? Ken says I'm always putting my foot in it."

" She's my tenant, not my friend."

" Oh, that's different, I can say what I like then, and I think she's a bitchy old bag. She was always dropping in to see Mr. Begbie and none of us girls could stand her, she treated us like dirt. What Aunt Agnes can see in her—you know Aunt Agnes, don't you? Miss Turnberry. She lives over the butcher's in the High Street."

"Yes, I have three of her dolls. I didn't realise she was your aunt."

"Frightful old gossip, isn't she?" said Margery with cheerful candour. "I don't go and see her as much as I ought, her chitter-chatter drives me nuts, but she's a nice old dear really and I hate to see her under Sibley's thumb. Do this, run and fetch that—you'd think the ghastly woman owned her. Haven't you noticed it?"

"I haven't spoken to either very much lately."

"It was old Sibley, you know, who landed us with that damned cat." There was real bitterness in her tone now. "And I don't know for sure, but I think she put up some of the money to build this place. The land is Ken's but that's all, we didn't have any say in the cottage or I'd have made them put in a bathroom. I mean, copying the other is all very well but there are limits. An outside loo in this day and age! And an earth-closet at that, can you believe it?"

"It does seem like carrying things to extremes," agreed Miss Purdy thoughtfully. "Of course, you're a bit far out for mains."

"Yes, but you'd have thought they could have managed *something*. Water too—we have to use an old well at the back and it was no joke back in February, I can tell you. I'll bet old Dillinger wouldn't put up with it himself."

"Oil lamps too, I see."

"Ken suggested a generator but they wouldn't have it at any price. Spoil the atmosphere, they said, and that's why we're stuck with this old furniture too." She looked around with a dissatisfied expression. "Not my taste at all, give me whitewood and a nice cheerful carpet every time, but Mr. Begbie said—"

"Mr. Begbie too?"

"Oh yes, a whole gang of them, they're dead interested

in having the period right. We shouldn't have got the place if we hadn't agreed."

Though strongly against anything that savoured of blackmail, Miss Purdy had to admit that whoever had furnished the cottage had done so with considerable taste. Nothing pretentious or out of keeping; a simple oak dresser, square table and rush-seated chairs which might believably have grown old with the cottage. A rag rug covered the flags in front of the range, a couple of stained and faded watercolours of Witchwater and the surrounding marshes relieved the whitewashed walls, and a Victorian tea-service brightened the shelves above the built-in cupboard beside the hearth. She wondered if 'they' had seen the portable TV set on a brand-new coffee-table in the corner, which provided the only jarring note. Margery saw her looking at it and read her expression correctly.

"No, they don't know we've got it, Ken only bought it a couple of weeks ago. I suppose he shouldn't have, but I said I'd go mad if we didn't have something to show we're alive. Tell you the truth—" she looked around her a little uneasily—" it's a nice cottage and I know it's really new but I sometimes feel there's something *screwy* about it. Don't you?"

" Screwy?"

" Oh, I don't mean the witchcraft crap, but that girl—what's her name? Jessica—after all she *was* murdered here, and it doesn't seem right to make the place look as though she was going to walk in any minute and turn us out. And as for that damned Elimauzer—"

" Who called him that?" asked Miss Purdy sharply.

She pulled a face. " The Sibley bitch, who else? I can't stand the brute but we've got to give him a home, it's in the agreement."

Miss Purdy set her tea-cup down with care. " Tell me, Margery, these people ruling your lives—who are they?"

33

" The Antiquarian Society. You know, dead nuts on history and folk-lore and local legends, that sort of thing. Begbie and Dillinger and Sibley and old Wetherby—"

" Wetherby—the bookseller in the High Street?"

" Yes, he sort of started it, I think. Nasty little creep, isn't he? But there are *some* nice members. Ken's boss, Major Barlow, for one. You must have heard of him—he lives at Bilby Hall—"

" Oh yes, I've heard of him," said Miss Purdy drily. She refrained from adding that her informant was Inspector Lovick, who considered him a pompous old fool. " He owns a private helicopter, doesn't he?"

" Ken's his pilot," said Margery with pride. " He was in the Rescue Service, you know. He's got medals for it."

Miss Purdy was suitably impressed. " But Bilby Hall— that's several miles on the other side of Wrexley. A long way to commute."

" Oh, not so bad now they've lent us a motor-boat. There's a cut from here to the river and he leaves the boat at Wrexley Staithe and gets a bus the rest of the way. He wouldn't leave me here alone at night."

" I should think not, indeed." Miss Purdy paused as a slight cloud crossed her companion's expressive face. She said gently : " Is Major Barlow a good boss?"

" Oh yes, he's all right, it's just that—" Her friendly grin broke out again. " I'm being silly, that's all. Have you met Suzi Barlow?"

" I've heard about her," said Miss Purdy cautiously.

" Is she as pretty as they say?"

" I've never seen her to my knowledge. The major's granddaughter, isn't she? I was told she's here on a rest-cure."

" Ken says it's drugs. She got herself in a proper mess in London—some pop-star or other—it was in the papers—"

34

"That sort of thing doesn't interest me."

Margery made another grimace. "So long as it doesn't interest Ken either. . . . That's what I'm afraid of. No, forget it, I don't really mean—it's just that I've got the feeling she's making a play for him. Not seriously, of course—we're not her class—but he's very good-looking and being at the Hall all day—well, it makes you wonder, doesn't it? Especially when he's late home. Two o'clock it was last night and honestly, I was beginning to get the creeps. Well, I mean—all alone in this screwy place—"

"I don't blame you," said Miss Purdy strongly. "Two o'clock! He should have had more sense."

"Mind you, I'm not saying he could help it, it's his job after all, but I don't like her giving him orders and that's the truth. Last night it was making him take her over to Newmarket in the chopper just to see this pop-star—he's got racing-stables there or something—I'd like to give her racing-stables! I was hopping mad at the time but—oh well, I suppose he couldn't very well have refused." She blinked twice and sat up straight. "Like I said, I'm being silly, so let's talk about something else. Another cup of tea?"

"No, thank you, dear, I enjoyed that but I must be going." She stood up. "I can't say I'm very enamoured of your Antiquarians."

"Oh, they're not all nasty, Aunt Agnes for one, she can't help being a bit loopy. You should see her cooing over Elimauzer! Though how she can bear to touch him—"

"Where did his silver collar come from?"

"He was wearing it when they brought him here. It's ever so old, you know. Mr. Dillinger says it's quite valuable."

"I'm surprised they let him run wild with it, then."

"So am I, daft I call it. Ken made it quite clear we

wouldn't be held responsible."

"Very wise." Miss Purdy paused in the act of picking up her coat. "My dear, your husband—you said he owned this land. Do you mean he bought it?"

"Oh no, he inherited it, didn't you know? That girl who was murdered—Jessica—he's some sort of cousin of hers."

Miss Purdy stood very still. "I thought she was the last of the line."

"So did everybody else till Mr. Begbie got busy. He was her solicitor, you see, and it was his job to find an heir, so he looked up dozens of old records and found this other lot in Plymouth. Funny how things turn out, isn't it? Jessica's great-grandfather had a brother who moved down there over a hundred years ago and Ken's the last one left. Surprise of his life to find he'd come into a bit of property, even though there wasn't any money to go with it." She giggled suddenly. "The joke is, he's always been a bit of a Commie, ranting on about the System and heads rolling and Come the Revolution and all that crap. Silly really because you couldn't want anyone kinder, and when it comes to dinner it's all I can do to make him kill a chicken."

"How did he like the idea of owning property?"

"He didn't. Mr. Begbie had a hard job persuading him even to come and look at it, and what with its being out in the wilds and practically unsaleable—" She giggled again. "He near as anything turned tail and went home again, so Mr. Begbie put me to work on him. We sort of clicked right from the start, and when they suggested rebuilding the cottage here—well, it was all we'd ever prayed for and there was never any question after that. Soon as it was finished we got married and moved in. Like a fairy story, isn't it? Except—"

Her pretty face clouded as she looked round the

pleasant old-fashioned room.

"Except what?" prodded Miss Purdy gently.

"I do wish they'd put in a bathroom," said Margery discontentedly.

But Miss Purdy had the feeling she'd been about to say something quite different.

CHAPTER THREE

Inspector Lovick, too, had spent most of the morning on the marshes but in a different direction—over towards Bilby Heath on the western outskirts of his manor. And he hadn't enjoyed it. He was getting too old for these capers. April sunshine was all very well, but when you were overweight with high blood pressure and your missus hadn't let you leave off your winter woollies—well, he for one could do without it, especially on a day entailing leg-work over these flaming marshes.

Not that he'd anticipated legwork on setting out, otherwise he'd have left things to Donzell, the sergeant on the spot, giving him a chance to display that ruddy efficiency he was so proud of. Trouble was he'd clean forgotten that the tatty old ruins of St. Edred's lay a good mile-and-a-half from the nearest negotiable road. Once upon a time St. Edred's had been a flourishing abbey on the edge of a good fishing-broad with a fine run down to the river, and he wouldn't mind betting those monks had done themselves a good deal better in the way of approach-roads than the present Council, if only to get the produce of field and fishery to Norwich market and earn themselves some holiday-money. Progress! True, the silting up of broad and tributary and the reduction of the abbey to a few crumbling walls, a tombstone or two and a corner of highly dangerous roof had lessened the need for ready access, especially as the nearest village was more than two miles distant, but this didn't alter the fact that the police-car hadn't been able to get within spitting-distance and the rest of the journey had had to be made on foot. If only someone had warned him before he'd set out—

But the whole thing had been sprung on him without warning. The manor had been remarkably free from trouble for some weeks and he'd arrived at the station after breakfast expecting nothing more strenuous than some placid paperwork, with perhaps a side-trip to Miss Purdy's if he felt like it to find out why she'd been blathering about smells. Instead, he'd been confronted by the desk-sergeant relaying an urgent report from Donzell.

" Spot of trouble over at St. Edred's, sir. Donzell's just been through."

" What sort of trouble?"

" Well—"

" Is it a secret?"

" No, sir."

" Then stop waffling and spit it out."

The sergeant's hesitation was due to years of experience of Lovick's two pet phobias—Donzell and hanky-panky. Having to present him with both at once would have shaken the strongest nerves. ' Hanky-panky ' in Lovick's dictionary usually meant the supernatural. This business didn't exactly fit into that slot but it had a nasty flavour, all the same, and it was odds on Lovick would run true to form.

He did.

" Say that again," he ordered dangerously.

" Black magic, sir. At least—"

" Has Donzell gone bonkers?"

" No, sir, but what with these tombstones shifted and some sort of altar rigged up—"

" At *St. Edred's*?"

" Yes, sir. This marshman called Blofield was on his way to work and—"

" Get me a car."

" Yes, sir."

And with the steaming intention of sorting out this crap once and for all, Lovick had immediately leapt—well, inserted his bulk—into the passenger-seat and snapped out an order to be taken to the scene pronto.

And what he'll say when he finds he has to get out and walk, thought the desk-sergeant—

The easiest way would have been to go by boat, but even a desk-sergeant can't think of everything. It was five minutes before he could stop laughing.

Lovick wasn't laughing on arrival. He was hot and he was tired. Donzell, on the other hand, was hopping fresh and sizzling with his usual dratted efficiency, itching to clear away inessentials like inspectors and get on with the job.

" Not kids, sir," he reported smartly. " More serious than plain vandalism. Take a look at those flagstones. Strength needed to prise 'em up, let alone lift that big one and prop it over the others. And if you'll look around—"

" I'm trying to, aren't I? Shut up and let me form my own impressions."

Sitting down heavily on a convenient chunk of masonry, he surveyed the scene with jaundiced eyes.

Must be all of ten years since he was last this way. Place hadn't changed much. Bit more gone from the south wall, perhaps, but you could still see traces of a window opposite and stumps of old pillars thrusting up among the grass and weeds.

Ah, that willow-tree. Ten years ago it had been a mere sapling shoving a tentative frond or two through a gap in the wall over to his left. Now it was fifteen foot high or more, leaning over the top like a woman on washing-day to see what was going on. Through another gap he could see the marshes over which he'd just traipsed, stretching out to eternity under a vast pale-blue sky across which a couple of marsh-harriers were wheeling.

Lonely was the right word. Place gave him the willies. Funny, it hadn't done that last time, he'd rather enjoyed the solitude. Sat in this very spot if he remembered rightly, chewing ham sandwiches and washing 'em down with a can of beer. But now—

Ignoring Donzell and the old marshman hovering in the background, his gaze travelled towards the east end. Not much left of that part. Tumbled masonry, the ghost of an arched doorway, a crazy step or two and a clear view to a horizon which probably embraced the North Sea. Yet that was where the biggest change was evident. Broken flagstones had been piled in two rough heaps where once a genuine altar had stood, and a larger slab still bearing faint traces of an inscription had been manhandled to lie across them. And what the devil were those flakes of black?

Lumbering heavily to his feet, he went over to inspect this fresh obscenity at close quarters.

" You see, sir?" said Donzell eagerly from close behind him. " Cock feathers!"

Lovick jerked away. " Don't breathe down my neck."

" No, sir. But those black feathers—"

" I've got eyes."

" Some heathen sacrifice took place here last night," said Donzell impressively, " and if that isn't blood I'll eat my hat." He pointed to a dark stain on the ' altar ' top.

" Taken a sample for the lab?"

" Of course, sir. First thing."

His ruddy efficiency again. Never missed a blasted trick. Not that the cock-feathers took much finding. Some on the slab and more scattered around on the grass-grown flag-stones. No doubt he'd got some tucked away in an envelope too, just to prove they hadn't been dropped by an absent-

41

minded peacock.

Something else caught Lovick's eye. Stepping right up to the slab, he bent forward to peer at it closely. Splashes of something dark—waxy—faintly glistening—

" Candle-grease, sir," said Donzell inevitably. " *Black* candle-grease." He gave the word ' black ' a suitably sinister emphasis. " Which I think you'll agree settles it. This place was used last night for devil-worship."

Lovick looked at his sandy-haired, sharp-nosed subordinate without affection. " You're supposed to be in charge round here. How long have devils been roaming round your patch?"

" S-sir!" As always when taken aback, Donzell began to hiss and splutter. " This is the first—I never s-s-suspected—"

" Don't spit at me. When was this discovered?"

" Half-past s-six this morning, sir. Ted Blofield here—"

" Any idea who's responsible?"

" Not yet, sir, but—"

" Four whole hours? You must be slipping."

He turned his attention to Ted Blofield, a typically slow-speaking, slow-moving marshman who gave the impression of being slow-witted too. Lovick, Norfolk-born and bred himself, knew this was misleading. Your true marshman took a lot of beating for wisdom and acumen, let alone sheer stoical guts. This chap must be nearing eighty but his back was as straight as any city bloke's half his age, and Lovick would have given a lot for some of the shrewdness and know-how inside that snow-white head. Beside him, Donzell was a smart-alec, a rattlepate, and Lovick's tone altered accordingly.

" 'Morning, Ted."

" 'Mornin', sir. Reckon this be a dirty business an' no mistake."

" Anything like it happened before?"

42

"Not as I ever heerd on. Them stones wor all right yesterday, I'll take my oath. Reckon they took a bit o' shiftin' too. More'n one man's job."

"I don't doubt it. You're working near here?"

"Ay, sir, clearin' out the dykes from all their winter muck, by which token them varmints, whoever they be, they been at my tools." He pointed towards an obscure corner where a small section of low roof provided hazardous protection from the weather. Dydle and crome—both dyke-clearing tools—leant against the wall with a spade lying on the ground near by, but it wasn't these he was concerned about. "It's my old besom, sir, can't see her nowhere an' I reckon them danged so-and-sos ha' made off wi' her."

For a bemused second Lovick had the impression he was referring to his wife, but Donzell put him right.

"His twig broom, sir."

"Anything else missing?"

"Not so far as he knows."

Lovick looked at Blofield. "Get many visitors out here?"

"Not out o' season, sir. One or two historical gentlemen, mebbe—oh ay, an' that Anti—Anti-suffin' Society—"

"Wrexley Antiquarian Society," supplied Donzell smartly.

"That's right, takin' photographs an' such. Then there wor an American lady an' her man—gi' me five pun for showin' 'em round these here mucky stones an' tellin' 'em all about St. Edred."

"What do you know about St. Edred?" demanded Lovick.

The old man gave a sudden throaty chuckle. "Dang-all, mister, an' that's a fact, but it makes a powerful good story—the devil hisself a-draggin' him down in that there pool an' the air-bubbles still risin' to prove it."

"Marsh-gas, you old sinner, and well you know it."

"Don't sound nigh so purty, callin' it marsh-gas."

43

Donzell (a staunch Presbyterian) clucked disapprovingly, which immediately made Lovick (C. of E.) feel better. But this was no time for fun and games. Turning his back on both of them, he took a closer look at the terrain.

'More'n one man's job' was an understatement. If he was any judge, at least a dozen people had tramped about the ruins last night, inside and outside the walls, but the squelchy turf took no clear impressions, and where patches of mud might have been more helpful, deliberate attempts had been made to destroy outlines. The most that could be deduced was that the footprints included at least one set of high heels, which come to think of it was interesting in its own right, quite apart from what the woman had been doing here.

How in heck had she reached this god-forsaken spot? Not by teetering over nearly two miles of lumpy, spongy marshland, that was certain; she'd have broken her ankle in less than fifty yards. Cars were out of it. A motor-cruiser bringing her up-river from Wrexley—

He stopped to kick himself, metaphorically. Why hadn't he thought of that for himself this morning? Or rather, why hadn't that blockheaded desk-sergeant thought of it for him? Saving him a good mile and more of—

Oh well. The woman. Even if she'd had more sense than the desk-sergeant, she'd still have faced more foot-slogging than you can do on high heels. The silting up of the abbey fishing-broad (except for that pool Ted had just mentioned) had left the ruins not exactly high or dry, but well beyond spitting-distance from the river. Technically, he supposed, you could propel a punt along the dyke Ted had been clearing, but the mental picture this conjured up seemed highly unlikely. Yet how else—

Broomstick, he thought sourly, and immediately cursed himself for pandering to the fool ideas Donzell had dreamed up with his blessed cock-feathers. Witchcraft and black

44

magic were bunk. Lot of silly perverts playing at—

At this point, a distant sound in the sky began to impinge on his consciousness and he looked up, startled, almost expecting a high-heeled witch on a broomstick to materialise, but all he saw was a rapidly-approaching helicopter.

Behind him, Donzell gave a satisfied grunt. " Major Barlow, sir. He brought me out here, promising to pick me up in time for lunch."

Lovick spun round to face him, his cheeks turning slightly purple. " You mean you didn't *walk* here?"

" No, sir. Waste of time when Major Barlow—"

" Major Barlow," said Lovick distinctly, " is a pompous old blabbermouth, and you're a ruddy sight too friendly with him."

Donzell began to stutter again. " S-sir—p-public relations—p-part of my p-policy—"

" Policy be damned, you're a blasted snob. Just because he lives at Bilby Hall—" He conquered the worst of his feelings with an effort, but remained dangerously official. " So help me, if he's spilt any of this to the Sunday papers—"

" I warned him to keep his mouth shut."

" He doesn't need a mouth, it oozes out of his ears."

At least nobody could doubt the major's enthusiasm. A boisterous waving from the passenger-seat began long before it had any chance of being seen, and the machine had barely grounded when he clambered out as agilely as a youngster half his age, his rosy-cheeked boyish face alight with eager good-will.

" Hullo, hullo, hullo! 'Morning, Inspector! Lucky your sergeant here called me in. Woke me out of a good sleep to do it but always ready for a bit of Sherlocking, what? Wait till you hear my report! Knew I'd be able to help you!"

Donzell did the mental equivalent of grinding his teeth.

If the old fool had indeed been Sherlocking—

Though proud of his carefully-cultivated friendship with the wealthiest land-owner on his patch and the only possessor of a private helicopter for miles around, he sometimes doubted if the ensuing advantages were worth the agonies of embarrassment springing from the major's scatterbrained enthusiasm, and now he was sure of it. They weren't. The major had been up to something. Success shone out of him like neon lighting. After the strictest injunctions to keep this under his hat—the sergeant almost groaned aloud.

Trust him to come out with it in front of Lovick.

Lovick, however, was thinking the old fool didn't look quite as rosy-cheeked as of yore and that the enthusiasm seemed a trifle less spontaneous. Distinct bags under the eyes when you looked closely and his sports-jacket hung on him as if he'd lost weight. Now he came to think of it there'd been mention of a slight heart-attack fairly recently, and all that gossip about the grand-daughter couldn't have helped—hot bit of goods there all right—

Then the major's last remark registered and he stiffened ominously. " You say you can help us, sir?"

The major beamed at him. " Those cock-feathers, Inspector. Tied up in knots, eh? Wondering where they came from."

" I know where they came from," said Lovick repressively.

The beam gave place to chagrin. " You do?"

" A cock."

" Ah, but *whose* cock?" A waggish finger was waved under his nose. " If you can tell me that—"

" Look, sir, if you've been spreading this affair all round the village—"

" Not a word, Inspector, mum as the grave. Dropped in my lap as you might say. In the shop for 'baccy and there she was, blathering to all and sundry—nearly in tears,

46

poor woman—well, stands to reason—counting on him for dinner—"

"What woman, Major?" broke in Donzell before his superior could develop apoplexy.

"Ah, Donzy, old boy! Old Mrs. Pegg, of course. End cottage past the pond."

"Yes, yes, I know her."

"Kicking up the devil of a fuss, poor soul. Fox got into the coop during the night and stole her black rooster. So of course I—"

"Told her it wasn't a fox," said Lovick acidly.

The major looked hurt. "Not at all, Inspector, not at all. Never breathed a syllable. Simply warned her not to go near the coop as the sergeant here might be round to take fingerprints."

"Of a *fox*?"

"Well, over seventy—seemed only fair to—oh!" The major rubbed his button of a nose. "See what you mean, Inspector. Boobed a bit there, I'm afraid. Still—" His face brightened. "Not to worry! Make a point of calling there this afternoon to say I was thinking of poachers, not foxes. Simple!"

"You'll do nothing of the sort, sir. You've done quite enough already, and I'm grateful. Only one thing more, if you don't mind. I'd like a lift to my car."

"Certainly, certainly, anything you say. Come back for you later, Donzy, old boy. All right?"

"No," cut in Lovick before the sergeant could speak. "He'll be busy here for some time yet and he can find his own way home. And don't forget to include those dabs in your report," he instructed Donzell maliciously.

"Dabs, sir?"

"On the chicken-coop."

Five minutes later, squeezed between the rotund major and the wooden-faced young pilot, Lovick waited until his

47

stomach had settled after take-off and then glanced at the pilot with curiosity. "Not seen you before in these parts, have I?"

"No, sir," said the young man briefly.

The talkative major cut in. "Only had him a few months, Inspector, and don't know what I'd do without him. Chauffeur, pilot, general dogsbody—worth your weight in gold, eh, Ken?"

"I do my best, sir."

"How's that pretty young wife of yours?"

"Very well, sir, thank you."

"Given up piloting myself," the major confided to Lovick wistfully. "Doctor's orders. Heart. Hated it at first— someone else at the controls—never could stand being a passenger. But young Ken there—trust your life with him. Ah! That your car down there?"

Glad to be on firm ground again, Lovick shook the major's hand with the first genuine cordiality he'd felt towards him.

"Thanks for the lift, sir. Very grateful. But no more amateur sleuthing, right? Or I'll have to have a word with your doctor. I'm sure he'll agree excitement's bad for you."

"And you'll both be wrong," retorted the major with unexpected spirit. "Puts a bit of spice into life. Might as well be dead as sit at home doing nothing."

"Then I'll have to rely on this young man to keep you in order." Lovick turned to the pilot. "Didn't catch your last name."

"Kenneth Daw, sir."

"Daw!" A memory stirred. "I knew a Daw not far from here once, but—no, can't be any connection, she was the last of 'em, and a good thing too. You living with the major?"

For the first time a brief smile touched the young man's lips. "No, sir. At Witchwater."

Lovick's jaw dropped. " Witchwater! But that's where—
you can't mean you're—"

" Jessica was a sort of cousin."

Lovick's mouth was still open as the machine whirred
skyward.

CHAPTER FOUR

Arriving home just before lunch. Miss Purdy found a furniture-van outside the house, the front door standing wide open and a man in a brown overall going upstairs. He could hardly have reached the first landing when two others lumbered down from the top floor humping a divan-base between them. Above them peered the anxious face of David Carter.

Seeing her, he followed the men down and tapped at her sitting-room door before entering.

"Sorry about this, Miss Purdy," he began wretchedly. "Bit of a mix-up, they've come a day early."

"So I see."

"Shirley's upstairs crying her eyes out. Now it's come to the point—"

"Has she changed her mind?"

"No, she still can't face staying, she just wishes she could. If only that damned woman hadn't mentioned spooks—" He stopped, running a hand through his thick dark hair. "Anyhow, I want you to know we're both sorry to go. None of it's your fault. The flat was our idea of heaven until—oh heck, what can I say? Except thank you. From Shirley as well as me."

Miss Purdy was touched. "Would you like to stay to lunch?"

"That's very kind of you but—no. Sooner we get away the better. Wish us luck finding a new place, will you?

Personally I'd rather face spooks than an overdose of Shirley's mother."

When they and the van had finally gone, Miss Purdy went up to the top flat and walked from room to room. The Carters had left it clean and completely empty. A simple, pleasant flat, warm and convenient, ideal for a childless couple. And not a trace of smell . . . I can't afford to let it stand empty, she thought, staring across rooftops at the sparkling surface of Wrexley Broad. But I will *not* let it to friends or relations of Mrs. Sibley under any circumstances, and if I can get rid of her too I will. Not through Mr. Begbie, he's too involved personally. If Inspector Lovick can't help me, I'll find another solicitor.

Halfway down the bottom flight she heard the middle-flat door open and wished heartily she'd started downstairs a few seconds earlier. She was in no mood for a confrontation before she'd had her lunch. Luck, however, was on her side for once; the phone in Mrs. Sibley's flat began ringing and the stout, overdressed figure didn't appear. Greatly relieved, Miss Purdy skipped into sanctuary and went through to the kitchen, but she didn't breathe easily until the front door closed and she was sure she had the house to herself.

Half an hour later, just as she'd settled down to do the *Times* crossword, the phone on her own desk rang and she picked it up with a sigh of impatience. " Miss Purdy here."

" Oh, Miss *Purdy*!" She knew that italicised voice; it belonged to Miss Turnberry, the doll-maker, Margery Daw's elderly Aunt Agnes, whose only vices—as far as Miss Purdy knew—were talking too much and being friendly with Mrs. Sibley. Another sigh escaped her. She was in for a long session. Miss Turnberry was as voluble on the phone as off it, a godsend to the financially-embarrassed Post Office but not to her unfortunate acquaintances.

51

True to form, the italics continued. "*Dear* Miss Purdy! Do *please* forgive me for interrupting—you authors—so very clever—I know it's *dreadful* of me but—"

"Not at all," said Miss Purdy as civilly as possible. "I'm not actually working at the moment. If I can help you—"

"Oh, you can, you can! Sibyl—Mrs. Sibley—do you know if she's out? I've been ringing and ringing all morning but there's no reply. And she *promised*—"

"She was in half an hour ago."

"Oh dear! Then it must be the *phone* out of order, though there was nothing wrong with the ringing sound. You don't think she's been taken *ill*?"

"I'm sure she hasn't. I heard her come downstairs and the front door shut. Are you sure you dialled the right number?"

"Oh yes, yes, yes! I *couldn't* go wrong about that. Such a *very* dear friend—"

"Well, the phone was working just before she left. She went back to answer it."

"But that's *incredible*! I tried a dozen times at least. I suppose you've no idea where she's gone?"

"Not the slightest, I'm afraid."

"Then it's too late," said Miss Turnberry tragically. "Oh, Miss Purdy! What—*what* am I to do?"

What Miss Purdy should have done (as she told herself afterwards) was to have murmured something non-committal and rung off, knowing that tragedy to Miss Turnberry could mean anything from a cracked tea-cup to a slug on her lettuce. But it wasn't in her nature to refuse help (or, as Lovick would have put it, to resist meddling) and it must be admitted curiosity did play a part in keeping the receiver to her ear.

"To do about what?" she enquired, trying to sound neutral.

"The Antiquarian Society—this lecture in Norwich—

Sibyl was to pick me up after breakfast and drive me over. Shopping and lunch and then—and I was *so* looking forward to it—not the shopping but the lecture—an American professor, can you believe it? Talking about Salem and those dreadful—but it starts at three and I've no car and the bus has gone and now I shall *miss* it. I could *cry* with disappointment!"

The last word was swallowed up by something between a hiccup and a sob. Miss Purdy hesitated and was lost. "If that's all, would you like me to drive you over?"

"Oh, Miss Purdy! I couldn't—shouldn't—would you *really*? There'd be just time if we start at *once*."

"I'll get the car out straight away," said Miss Purdy with resignation.

It certainly wasn't how she'd have chosen to spend the afternoon. On the other hand, her interest had already been aroused by the Antiquarians' connection with Witchwater, and although Miss Turnberry's company was a heavy price to pay for this chance of making their acquaintance, it did mean the outing wouldn't be a total loss.

As she put on hat and coat, she paused a moment to eye the Shirley doll, sitting primly and properly behind the glass paperweight. So much for Mrs. Sibley's prediction, she thought; the girl had gone, but she was still safe and well. They were halfway to Norwich before she realised the woman hadn't specified *whose* death was in question. . . .

The lecture about witch-hunting in seventeenth-century Massachusetts was genuinely interesting and Miss Turnberry sat enthralled throughout, her long thin nose glowing with radiance, her fingers clasped against her skinny chest in an attitude of adoration. Miss Purdy enjoyed it too in a more detached way, and as they walked together afterwards to the hotel where tea had been arranged she brushed aside her companion's garrulous and quite disproportionate thanks.

" The gratitude's on my side for an unexpected treat. But I wonder why Mrs. Sibley wasn't there? If she was as keen on the lecture as you say—"

" And not to *tell* me!" Miss Turnberry became agitated again. " It *can't* be illness if you saw her going out. And not even to answer the phone! I can't understand—"

" Perhaps she mistook the date," suggested Miss Purdy sensibly. " It happens to the best of us."

The Antiquarians had booked a private room and between twenty and thirty members were assembling there, highly-respected middle-aged people for the most part, with a good sprinkling of elderlies. Wrexley's upper crust, she thought ironically—the vicar, one of the local doctors, the headmistress of a large private school, businessmen and their wives, a few shopkeepers and farmers, with wealthy oddities like Major Barlow and near-penniless oddities like Miss Turnberry leavening the stodge.

Harvey Dillinger, the builder, came over to her at once. A stout and genial widower, he'd have been a dead ringer for Henry the Eighth if the latter had been able to patronise the Norwich equivalent of Carnaby Street for his clothes. Allowing her hand to be crushed by his, she felt slightly embarrassed by the fact that she'd declined his tender for central-heating and given the job to his ex-partner, but he didn't appear to bear malice. His friendliness, in fact, was overpowering, and he made a great point of introducing the girl he was escorting, Suzi Barlow.

" The major's grand-daughter," he said expansively. " You know Major Barlow, of course—over there talking to the vicar."

" I've heard of him," agreed Miss Purdy warily, remembering some of Lovick's unrepeatable epithets for the gentleman. " And of you too, Miss Barlow. I've no right to be here, I'm afraid—I mean, I'm not a member of the Society, simply a substitute-chauffeur for Miss Turnberry, whose friend Mrs. Sibley doesn't seem to have turned up."

"Funny, that," said Dillinger. "Usually one of our keenest members."

Somebody distracted his attention for a few moments, leaving Suzi and Miss Purdy to eye each other with mutual interest. So this is the potential husband-snatcher, thought Miss Purdy, not at all sure that Margery wasn't right to be worried. Suzi Barlow was an extremely pretty girl whose looks, most unfairly, had been given character by experiences that should have ruined them. Everybody in Wrexley knew about her suspended sentence in London for being in possession of cannabis, and there were rumours of at least one abortion (an activity still looked on askance in rural Norfolk) while the linking of her name with that of a well-known pop-singer had done nothing to lessen local interest. Yet she could have modelled for a painting of an only slightly dissolute Madonna. Dark blue eyes with deep purple shadows were set in a haggard face above a straight nose and soft full lips, and the skin of her high-boned cheeks was so pale as to be almost translucent against the black hair falling halfway to her waist. Her expression, half-defiant and half-whimsical, held a disturbing quality difficult to analyse, but at least through all her misdemeanours she'd kept a sense of humour.

"Bad luck, Miss Purdy. You're looking at the local Jezebel. Is it worth a couple of cream buns?"

"That depends," returned Miss Purdy cautiously. "How good are the buns?"

Suzi laughed outright. "Pretty foul, I expect. Let's try them and see."

Dillinger was with them again. "Bang on the button, sweetie, just what I was going to suggest." He steered them towards an empty table in the window. "And before we've finished, Miss Purdy, I hope to enrol you as a full-time member. Always on the look-out for new blood, you know.

55

Of the right type, of course. Have to keep the party congenial."

Miss Purdy looked around for her travelling-companion and found herself deserted. Miss Turnberry had joined three cronies at the other side of the room, her wispy yellow-white head bobbing non-stop as she treated them to a buzz-by-buzz account of her abortive efforts to get in touch with Mrs. Sibley this morning. Accepting her fate, Miss Purdy dropped into the chair being held for her by Dillinger and began to make polite conversation, helped by the arrival of the proprietor of Wrexley's only good bookshop, a dried-up little man of seventy-odd with whom she'd had many interesting encounters.

" No need for introductions." She smiled at him. " How do you do, Mr. Wetherby? I heard you were a member."

" Not just a member," said Suzi in mock reproof. " Mr. President himself. The Society couldn't exist without him."

" Oh, come now, Miss Barlow," said the little man modestly. " If you'd said without my books—"

" You *are* your books, and I mean that as a compliment. Have you seen his private collection, Miss Purdy? Not the stuff on show but the loot he keeps in his study? What they call a mine of local information. Any member is welcome to consult it."

" That sounds a great temptation."

" Knew we'd rope you in before we'd finished," said Dillinger, piling strawberry jam on to his toasted scone. " Wetherby's an authority, of course. We're doing St. Edred's next week. Ruined abbey on the marshes. How about it?"

But though genuinely tempted, it wasn't her way to be stampeded into anything, and the most he could extract from her was a promise to think it over.

" Talking of St. Edred's," began Suzi mysteriously, then stopped and looked at her sideways. " But I forgot, you're

56

a friend of the fuzz, aren't you? And Grandfather says it's all very hush-hush. Still, I don't see why I shouldn't tell you. They found evidence of witchcraft there this morning, cock-feathers and what-have-you—blood—candle-grease—the lot. Grandfather gave his pet sergeant a lift to the scene and then did some sleuthing on his own. Actually discovered whose bird it was—I call that pretty clever, don't you? Look at him now, still cock-a-hoop over it, telling the whole table about it in confidence just as he told me. The poor darling's always wanted to play Sherlock and it's no fun without an audience."

Miss Purdy glanced across the room. The major was at the next table to Miss Turnberry's and he certainly had his audience, not only his immediate neighbours but everyone within neck-craning distance.

Dillinger frowned. He seemed to have difficulty in holding back a caustic comment, but Wetherby chuckled throatily and demanded the rest of the story. "Go on, Suzi, you can't stop there. Whose bird was it?"

"Old Mrs. Pegg's in the village," said Suzi demurely.

"Well! She certainly looks like an old witch but St. Edred's—her arthritis—how in the world did she get there?"

"On a broomstick, probably. No, that isn't fair." Suzi gave a mock sigh. "It's a shame to tell the truth but she had nothing to do with it, the cock was stolen during the night without her knowledge. At least, that's her story—you can still believe in the broomstick if you want to. As far as the other culprits are concerned, the cops as usual are completely baffled, and that—excuse me, Miss Purdy—includes your fat friend Inspector Lovick, who was also on the scene this morning. Grandfather gave him a lift in the helicopter to save his corns."

Miss Purdy was neither amused nor impressed by this recital. Nor was Dillinger, who for once looked at the girl

57

as though he'd like to spank her. Wetherby, after a polite titter, took refuge in the murky depths of history, quoting extensively from a mediaeval manuscript containing references to St. Edred's in its heyday. Suzi herself smiled her slow, sexy smile and after a few moments, from the change on Dillinger's face, it was plain that her hidden left hand had found his knee.

It was Miss Purdy's turn to decide she needed a spanking. From the start it had been obvious that Dillinger was making a heavy play for her, and his present look of fatuous adoration was little short of obscene. Whether Suzi returned his affection or was merely amusing herself at his expense was another matter.

In any case Miss Purdy had had enough. Gathering gloves and handbag together, she was about to suggest a move when the whole scene was suddenly transformed. For no immediately apparent reason the girl turned white, her body went rigid and her eyes glazed with terror. Then, without warning, her chair jarred back and she was on her feet, screaming.

"Turn it out! Get rid of it or I'll kill the bloody thing! Do you hear me? I—I—can't—can't—breathe—"

Gasping and retching, she clutched at her throat, her eyes dark with that terrible panic while a stunned and silent room looked on helplessly. In the middle of the silence a faint mewing sound was heard and Miss Purdy, looking round, saw a tiny ginger kitten rubbing itself against Miss Turnberry's leg. Major Barlow moved first. Scooping the kitten up he flung it violently through the nearest doorway and slammed the door shut, stopping to mop his brow before hurrying to his grand-daughter's side.

"All right, all right, my dear, it's gone now. If I'd seen it earlier—" He mopped his brow again, looking round at the company apologetically. "Can't stand cats, poor kid, never could, one of these phobias, you know? Only thing

58

to do is chuck the blasted thing out."

Miss Turnberry's voice rose shrilly above the renewed hubbub. "Major Barlow! Need you have been *quite* so rough? That poor little pussy! Such a sweet harmless—"

"Damn the woman," muttered Dillinger savagely. "Okay, Suzi darling, all over now. Let's get you out of here."

Still crying uncontrollably, Suzi was hustled out to the car-park between the two men, leaving the rest of the Antiquarians buzzing like an agitated bee-hive. It was several minutes before Miss Purdy could pluck Miss Turnberry from the swarm, get her into her own car and head for home. Miss Turnberry still had plenty to say about the major's summary ejection of the kitten, but after a few minutes she grew oddly silent, not rousing herself until they reached Wrexley.

Then she became agitated again. "*Dear* Miss Purdy, would you be *very* kind and drop me off at your own house? I *must* pop up to Mrs. Sibley's flat and find out what went wrong. No, don't bother to see me home afterwards. It's only a step and I shall be *quite* all right."

Taking her at her word, Miss Purdy dropped her at the front door and drove on round the corner to garage the car, feeling she'd had enough of Miss Turnberry for one day. But no, she might have known it; on her return the wretched woman was down in the hall again wringing her hands as usual.

"No lights back or front and *no* answer. Dear Miss Purdy, what can have happened to her? I have the most *dreadful* feeling—"

"Nonsense, it's not dark yet. She's probably gone to the pictures."

"She *never* goes to the pictures nowadays. All these naked people in bed—"

Miss Purdy pointed out rather tartly that 'Mary

59

Poppins' was the current attraction at the local cinema. "In any case, wherever she is it's her own business and I suggest you go home and have supper. When she does come back I'll give you a ring, and you can call her up or not as you choose."

Though she still thought Miss Turnberry's concern excessive, she was sufficiently infected by it to go upstairs before getting her own supper and knock and call on her own account. Without result. The flat remained as quiet as the grave.

The grave.

Why should that obvious and overworked cliche have sent an unpleasant ripple of prescience through her nerves? For heaven's sake! Was she becoming as morbidly theatrical as the Turnberry woman? Simply because a tenant was out of the house for a few hours—

She had a master-key but resolutely refused to consider using it, seeing no excuse for laying herself open to a charge of snooping. But she didn't enjoy her supper. Quite apart from Mrs. Sibley's comings and goings, it had been a puzzling and exhausting day. The rebuilding of Witchwater with such pernickety exactness seemed to her to have faintly sinister overtones, especially considered (rightly or wrongly) in conjunction with Suzi's report of some kind of black magic taking place at St. Edred's last night. She hoped to heaven the return of a Daw to the neighbourhood didn't presage a revival of that kind of mischief. On another level, she felt the departure of the young Carters as a personal loss as well as a completely unnecessary disaster from their point of view; they hadn't been here long but she'd enjoyed their company, and the circumstances of their going had been particularly galling. Then there was that queer business of Suzi Barlow and the ginger kitten. She didn't know the medical term for a pathological hatred of cats but she had too much sense to dismiss it as silly fancy;

phobias of any kind are as much an illness as mumps or appendicitis and cause just as much suffering. It would be a long time before she forgot the panic in the girl's eyes and the thin scream of hysteria in her voice. . . .

One thing, she decided, must be settled straight away—the cause of that intermittent smell upstairs and the erratic behaviour of the heating system. No use having Breck in again, and certainly not Dillinger. Putting away the last of the washing-up, she resolved to write a cheque for Breck without delay and have done with him before calling in an expert from Norwich.

Bill Breck himself modified this resolution by calling before she'd finished writing the cheque. After conventional greetings he followed her into the living-room, a tall, shambling middle-aged man in shabby pullover and slacks; he'd once been good-looking but the face under a shock of greying hair was now lined and harassed. As she poured out sherry for both of them, he eyed her with something like envy. Didn't know how lucky she was, he thought; this peaceful flat and not a worry in the world. He liked the look of her—neat grey-clad figure, clear complexion and smooth grey hair knotted back in an old-fashioned bun. They didn't make 'em like that any more. But his own troubles rushed back on him and he was frowning deeply when she handed him the glass.

"Your health, Mr. Breck."

"And yours, ma'am." They both drank. "I suppose you've guessed what I've come about?"

"Your cheque?" She gestured towards the desk. "I was just writing it."

"I wouldn't bother you so soon, but—" He looked into his glass for a moment in silence. Then his head jerked up. "Heck, you'll have to know sooner or later. I've had enough of Wrexley, Miss Purdy. I'm quitting."

"You mean giving up the business?"

61

" Clearing out altogether." His eyes were bleak. "One great big laugh for my old pal Dillinger, who'll have the field to himself. Mark my words, he'll be a millionaire before he's finished." His hand shook as he raised the glass to his lips again. "And I hope it chokes him."

Miss Purdy looked at him in real distress. People called him unreliable but she'd never heard anyone say he was lazy or unwilling, and he had a family to support. He was honest, well-meaning and—she was convinced—plain unlucky. The odd thing was, the bad luck hadn't started until the break-up of the partnership. Until then, if anything, he'd been the more respected of the two men, the one with the real expertise. Dillinger hadn't been much more than a good electrician. Yet since the split, Dillinger had prospered all along the line and Breck had had to fight hard for a livelihood.

He amplified this now. "Trouble is, I'm bad medicine. Ask anyone around here, job'll go wrong before I've been on it five minutes." He spoke with a kind of bitter hopelessness. "Oh, I'm cheaper than he is, I have to be to scrape a living at all, which is no doubt why you chose me. And what happened? Damned factory sends the wrong radiator, there's this ruddy smell the young lady complains about, floorboards have to come up again—"

" I'm sorry about that."

" Not half as sorry as I am, ma'am. Extra day's work for nothing, and don't tell me it might happen to anyone. Never happens to Harvey Dillinger, does it? Oh no, only to Muggins here." He drained the glass at a gulp. "And don't think you're the first to suffer. You're not."

His tongue loosened, he told her of other setbacks, some minor and some not. A bungalow he'd built for sale in the first flush of independence had fallen foul of a new road-scheme before the job was completed. An office extension had been held up for weeks by an unofficial strike in the

Midlands. His best workman had suffered permanent injuries from a fall off a ladder. Non-delivery of guttering on another job had lost him an important contract. Bad weather had held up a Council order. He'd only to touch a job for it to go wrong.

" Like that Midas bloke in reverse," he said with a bitter laugh. " But Dillinger—he's got the golden touch all right. I'd like to see him rot in hell."

" How long ago did you split up?"

" Couple o' years or so. I was a dead fool. Should ha' taken him to court, only—his wife—a decent lass—she was dying of cancer and I couldn't bring that on her too."

" Was the parting your idea or his?"

" Mine. You can't work with a man you can't trust. He bought this caravan site over Yarmouth way, see? On his tod. With his own money, so he said—nothing to do with me or the firm at all. Only he got behind with the payments and I found he'd borrowed the cash on the strength of the firm's name, not his, and was trying to diddle me out of my share. We had a right bust-up there in the office, but after that he got old Begbie to do most of the talking and that stumped me—you can't fight against lawyers—"

" I've always trusted Mr. Begbie," she told him rather sharply.

" More fool you, ma'am, if you'll excuse me. Not that I've any right—oh, he's fair enough as they go, I've naught else against him, but the way he and his tribe make black sound white—still, they wouldn't ha' got away with it so easy if it hadn't been for Harvey's missus. Salt o' the earth, she was, even if she couldn't talk posh. He used to fret about that, said it was holding him back, couldn't introduce her to the right people and all that. Damned snob. . . . Her mother kept a fish-and-chip shop and what's wrong wi' that? Well, she's gone now and they say he's got one o' the nobs in tow—the Barlow girl, no less. Never mind if she

63

dopes or sleeps around wi' half London so long as he can do his courtin' at the Hall. Makes me want to vomit."

"I hear he's rebuilt Witchwater," said Miss Purdy tentatively.

"Ay, and a nice little packet it's made him. Begbie was in on that too—and that witch o' yours upstairs—"

"*Witch*?"

"In a manner o' speaking." He corrected himself hastily. "Not meaning it literally, o' course—just her appearance, like. Put up most o' the money, so I hear. Whole gang makes me spit."

Miss Purdy felt she'd had enough. She signed the cheque and handed it to him. "What will you do now?"

"Oh, I'll get a job somewhere, I'm not afraid of that. I'm a good working builder and all the jinxes in the world can't take that from me. But I like being my own man, and I don't like giving Dillinger best. No bucking against Fate, though, is there?" He looked down at the cheque before folding it and putting it in his wallet. "Mighty good of you to let me have this so promptly. All right upstairs now?"

"Well, no. The Carters left this morning."

His face darkened. "My fault again."

"Nonsense, nobody's blaming you."

"They will," he prophesied with bitter emphasis. "Just give 'em time. Only I'll be gone where I can't hear 'em, thanks be. This bloody town gives me the creeps."

A good exit-line. It came back to her half-an-hour after his departure when the phone rang. Lovick's voice held an odd urgency. "Miss Purdy? That tenant of yours—when did you see her last?"

"Tenant—" But she had only one now, she remembered. Her voice sharpened. "You mean Mrs. Sibley?"

"That's right."

"Wait—I can't think—"

"Sit down if you're squeamish. This is bad news. We've

64

found her on the marshes. Dead."

"Dead!" She groped for the support of a chair-back. "But—how—"

He said savagely : " Fell off her blasted broomstick. Hold everything. I'm coming round."

CHAPTER FIVE

He was there in five minutes. She was badly shaken and still incredulous. " You weren't—serious—"

" Like heck I wasn't." He looked at the sherry, decided against it and took a short unofficial swig from his own brandy-flask. As an afterthought he offered the flask to her, but she shook her head. He put the flask back in his pocket. " Did you know she was missing?"

" Not missing, exactly. Out, yes. She went out just before lunch."

" You saw her? Spoke to her?"

" No, I was in the kitchen and heard the front door shut. That would be—oh, getting on for two, I can't say exactly. The top tenants had just moved out and—" The look in his eyes stopped her. " What have I said wrong?"

" Nothing, nothing at all—except that Doc. says she died last night."

She sat down heavily. " He must be mistaken."

" Grant's never mistaken. Couple of hours either side of midnight, that's his judgement. Whoever you heard leaving, it wasn't Mrs. Sibley."

She thought back through a daze of shock. Last night. . . . Hadn't Mrs. Sibley been at home last night? Until now she'd taken it for granted, but—

Now she couldn't say one way or the other. She hadn't got back from Norwich until after nine, and then—David Carter—and she'd gone to bed soon afterwards, her tired mind not registering either the usual upstairs sounds or the lack of them.

This morning? Witchwater till lunch-time, and then the fuss and bustle of furniture-removal which would have covered other sounds anyway. Nothing from the middle flat had left any imprint on her memory until after the Carters' departure when, coming downstairs after a tour of their flat, she'd heard Mrs. Sibley's door open and then the ringing of the phone. Somebody had gone back inside to answer it and a few minutes later the street door had shut, and there'd been no reason whatever for supposing 'somebody' to be anyone but Mrs. Sibley. . . .

She told Lovick all this with real distress. She hadn't liked the woman but blamed herself for not being more alert, especially for having done nothing about Miss Turnberry's unanswered phone calls.

"And then—when Mrs. Sibley didn't turn up at the lecture—I should have realised something was badly wrong. But Miss Turnberry always makes such a fuss about nothing. It's difficult to take her seriously."

But Miss Turnberry hadn't made a fuss about nothing this time. While Miss Purdy and her friends had been listening to a visiting professor and eating cream buns afterwards, Mrs. Sibley had been lying dead on the—

"Did you say on the marshes?"

Lovick nodded grimly. "Half a mile from St. Edred's, flat in the middle of nowhere. Dead as a doornail, every bone in her body smashed."

"But—what was she doing there?"

"Like I said, riding a ruddy broomstick, mother-naked except for a great black cloak. Oh, and a mask, if that counts. Hadn't forgotten her handbag, though; busted open when she fell, contents spilt all over the place. That's how we knew who she was."

His pale blue eyes were bleak. She hadn't been a pretty

sight by moonlight and acetylene-lamps, even with drifting mist doing its best to obscure the nastier details. . . .

For his second trip that day to those infernal marshes, he'd taken a leaf out of Donzell's book and commandeered the helicopter. Piloting had been a bit of a problem, Ken Daw having knocked off and gone home, but the ever-helpful major had quickly provided a substitute in the person of a neighbouring enthusiast. " Painting chap, ex-Navy, name of Stratton. Pal of Dillinger's, Fleet Air Arm together. Excellent pilot, takes a flip now and then to keep in practice, trust him with your life. Pick you up in ten minutes, right?"

Lovick didn't like painters on principle, and in his opinion Barlow was a sight too ready to trust other people's lives with his assortment of pilots, but Stratton won his approval by being punctual, clean-shaven, non-talkative and middle-aged; and this favourable impression was confirmed when it turned out he painted recognisable birds instead of incomprehensible abstract squiggles. Moreover, he hadn't poked his nose into police business when they'd got there but had stayed with the machine and waited patiently. Altogether an improvement on Barlow himself.

But when you'd said that, you'd said everything on the credit side of the excursion. Donzell's urgent radio-call had been passed on to Lovick just as the latter was sitting down to supper. Fate seemed to have a fixation about thwarting his taste-buds. Not that he'd minded very much on this occasion, as it turned out; toad-in-the-hole with cream trifle to follow wouldn't have been an ideal preamble to viewing this particular corpse, which Donzell, for all his blasted efficiency, had come across purely by accident. In other words, by getting lost.

" You see, sir," he'd explained as briskly as if he'd done something clever, " I thought it might pay to keep a watch on the abbey tonight in case those villains got up to their dirty tricks again, and I chose a roundabout way to get there to avoid being spotted."

" Spotted by what?" Lovick had asked sarcastically. " The great crested grebe?"

" They might have arrived early, sir. Only what with the mist and all—"

" You lost your way."

" Yes, sir. Visibility next to nil at times, and somehow I found myself following the wrong dyke. And then—this black hump on the ground—though actually I found her handbag first—"

Efficiency my left foot, Lovick now thought balefully. Serve him right, he'll have a bellyful of the wrong dyke, keeping watch over her till the team can get to work in daylight . . .

He became aware that Miss Purdy was looking slightly green. The first cushioning numbness of shock was wearing off and she'd begun to face details. She said with difficulty : " A—broomstick—"

" That's right, on the ground with her, snapped in half. Must have landed with her."

" Landed! You talk as if she was literally *riding*—"

" I'm talking of how it looks. There's no doubt she dropped from a good height. Every bone in her body—"

" Don't say that again. There *is* no height on the marshes. How could she possibly—"

" Don't ask me. Never ridden on a broomstick myself."

" What do you really think?"

" I—think—" he spaced the words precisely—" she was part of the fun and games at the abbey last night. May have been high on drugs—we'll know more about that after the autopsy. A besom's missing from Blofield's stuff; she could have spotted it and had the delusion she could fly. A lift-up in a plane or helicopter for a take-off and then—"

"Helicopter—Major Barlow's?"

"Not unless he and his grand-daughter are both lying. They swear it wasn't taken out last night."

"I think," said Miss Purdy faintly, "I'll have some of your brandy after all."

*　　*　　*

After ringing through for Dabs and a cameraman, he borrowed her master-key and went upstairs, saying he'd be back after he'd had a look at the place, and for the next half-hour she stayed where she was, listening to the trampling of official feet overhead and trying to assimilate what she'd been told.

Whatever the truth of her bizarre death, there seemed no reason to doubt that Mrs. Sibley had been at the heart of the revival of so-called witchcraft in the neighbourhood. She'd put up some of the money to rebuild Witchwater, she'd provided Elimauzer the cat and his traditional silver collar, she'd been present at the desecration of the abbey ruins last night. . . . And she's been living in my house, Miss Purdy thought, a shudder running through her. Eating, sleeping, weaving her black spells a few feet above my head. . . .

She closed her eyes, and against her will a picture of the dead woman began to build up in her mind with appalling clarity. Fifty-odd, almost squat, with heavy features and dyed black hair; hooded lids and brown hollows emphasising the beadiness of boot-button eyes; stout figure encased in over-bright colours and too many bits and pieces of expensive jewellery; thick ankles above fashionable, unsuitable shoes; all adding up to a plain middle-aged woman with more money than taste. But there'd been more, much more to her than that. You had to add a layer of malice and a dominating, almost hypnotic quality which, if you were caught off-guard, seemed to draw all the strength and will-power out of you, as she could testify only too well from their first meeting. She had no difficulty whatever in visualising her in a tall pointed hat and wind-bellied cloak riding between earth and stars on a conventional broomstick. She actually felt a cold draught blowing through the room, and the fire flickered and dimmed as though touched by a breath from another world. Absurd, of course, but she'd conjured up the woman's presence so vividly that she could almost hear the echo of her rasping voice and smell the sickly too-strong scent of gardenias that always clung to her. *She's trying to get through to me*, she thought dizzily, her senses beginning to swim in spite of the brandy. Trying to tell me something—something—oh no, don't let me hear it—

But it was worse than that. The room was fading out, she was sliding into a grey nothingness without light or warmth or limit and only the stifling smell of gardenias to link her to a half-forgotten reality. *She's trying to get hold of me.* That was the real horror. She was losing identity, being invaded, dispossessed, forced out of life into the grey limbo of formless mists that had no beginning and no end and—

The telephone rang.

The sudden clangour sent a shock-wave knifing through her, hurting unbearably and yet—she realised it with a choking sob of relief—expelling that other and giving her back to herself. The greyness dissolved, warmth and life came back, she was sitting in her own room again, whole and sane, and the wonderful, heavenly, eternally-blessed telephone was still ringing. . . .

Her shaking hand found the receiver. " Miss Purdy speaking." And how could she explain to this caller or to anyone else that it had so nearly *not* been Miss Purdy speaking, but a dead interloper?

" Oh, Miss Purdy !" Miss Turnberry's voice, urgent and

eager. "I've been waiting and *waiting*! Hasn't she come back yet? The most *dreadful* feeling—driving me frantic—I'm *sure* something's happened to her. Do you think—the police perhaps—"

"I'm sorry—no, she's not back, she—she's" Words died in her throat. What could she say? What could anyone say? Apart from the brutality of breaking such news on the phone to an elderly woman living alone, she didn't know if Lovick wanted it made public yet. Besides—her fingers closed tightly on the receiver—she still wasn't quite herself, and simply didn't feel capable of coping with the inevitable hysterics.

"Miss Purdy! Miss Purdy!" Shrillness was already evident. "Please—it isn't *kind* of you to keep me in suspense. If you'd only run up and *look*—make sure she isn't *ill*—I have this feeling, you see, and I'm so dreadfully *worried*."

"She's not in her flat." Miss Purdy's voice dragged unwillingly. "I'm quite sure of that, Miss Turnberry. I'll let you know the minute she—I—look, I'm sorry, really I am, but there's nothing I can do just now. Later—someone will be along to see you later."

She hung up, feeling wretchedly unsure of herself. Lovick, entering the room a few minutes later, was taken aback by her expression. "What in heck—aren't you well?"

"I can't stay here tonight."

"You'll be all right. Nothing here to—"

"No."

He looked at her still more closely. "Not like you to be scared. Who was that on the phone?"

"Miss Turnberry, but—"

"One who's been ringing up all day?"

"Yes, I promised to let her know when—Mrs. Sibley—"

72

His tone sharpened. " You tell her she's dead?" He looked relieved when she shook her head. " Okay, I'll send someone round. But about tonight—"

" I'll go to a hotel."

" Rubbish, we've a spare bed at home, the missus will be glad to see you. But why the big upset? Thought you didn't like your tenant."

" I didn't and don't. I'm sure she's evil. I can't explain and I hope you won't press me, but I shall be very grateful if you'll bear with me for a night or two, especially as the top floor is empty as well."

" Meant to ask you about that. Why did those kids leave? You said something about smells—"

" Do we have to go into it now?"

" I suppose it'll wait a few more minutes," he allowed grudgingly. " Meanwhile, if your legs are still working—"

She stood up to prove it.

" Good, then I'd like you to come upstairs and tell me what's missing. No obvious gaps but someone's definitely been rummaging around, probably the bloke you heard this morning, and if only you'd kept your eyes open then—" He broke off as she uttered a sudden exclamation. " Now what?"

" The man on the stairs!"

" What man?"

" When I got home from Witchwater, the Carters were already moving out. This man in a brown overall was just going up, and two others came down with a divan very shortly afterwards. I took all three for removal-men, but now I come to think of it only two drove away with the van. You can check with the firm, of course, but—"

" What firm was it?"

" ' Wrexley Removals '."

" Can you describe this bloke you saw?"

" Only his back. Tall, broad-shouldered, black hair

sprinkled with grey—sorry, I wasn't really noticing."

"That's what I'm complaining of." He jotted a note or two and returned the notebook to his pocket. "Fat lot of good this is, might even arrest myself on the strength of it. Still, you never know. . . . Anything else?"

"No, except that I'm wondering how he got in."

"No problem if he pinched her keys. We haven't found 'em yet. How well off was she?"

"Very comfortably, I think. Her husband owned a string of hardware shops in the Midlands, which she sold for a good sum."

He grunted. "Price of tools nowadays, I should have tried that lark myself. Anyway, judging by what's upstairs she invested most of it in jewellery, but that wasn't what this chap was after. Any ideas?"

She shook her head. He eyed her suspiciously. "Funny, you're usually bubbling over with 'em. What's scared you?"

"Nothing you would understand."

"Try me."

"Very well." She drew a long breath. "Just now—before the phone rang—she tried to—to take possession of me."

"She *what*?"

"I—I—please—I don't want to talk about it. Not yet."

"I might have known it," he said from the bottom of his heart. "Any jiggery-spookery and you're hooked. I suppose you're trying to tell me you believe in witchcraft."

"I believe in evil, and she frightens me more now than she did when she was alive. In the flesh I could make some attempt to deal with her. Now—" Her eyes glazed. Her hand went out blindly. "Don't leave me alone. Whatever you do, don't—don't leave me—"

"Here, stop it!" He caught hold of her hand, genuinely alarmed. "You can have the protection of the whole ruddy Force if you want it, though what use it'd be against—"

He gave up that line of thought. " Come on, let's get it over."

Surprisingly, she felt less vulnerable in the woman's own living-room than she had downstairs, though it took a strong effort of will to view the room objectively. She hadn't liked the re-decorations before and she didn't like them now. The high Victorian ceiling with its elaborate cornice had been shut off behind polystyrene tiles; the walls had been painted acid-green; curtains and loose covers, though expensive, clashed heavily with orange wall-to-wall carpeting; and various objets-d'art scattered lavishly about were—well, bizarre was the kindest word she could think of. A thin film of dust lay over everything, with a fingerprint expert busily adding to it, but there was no actual grime. Mrs. Sibley hadn't been a sleazy housekeeper, merely indifferent.

" Well ?" asked Lovick, watching her closely.

" I can't be of much help, I'm afraid. I wasn't in here often enough, two or three times at most. It looks just the same to me. Those drawers—" She nodded towards a set of half-open drawers forming part of a shelf-unit. " Were they like that when you—"

" No, but he'd been through them. Top one forced open and empty. Fifty-odd quid in another not touched."

She said suddenly : " That chair's been moved."

An armchair stood in the far corner, pushed well back. Lovick was about to ask how she knew when he saw the answer for himself, two deep impressions on the carpet where the front legs had stood habitually. This rubber-backed carpeting was a delusion and a snare to the ordinary unwary purchaser. Comfortable to walk on, good to look at and saved the expense of an underlay, but try putting heavy furniture on it and you were stuck. He should know, he'd been caught with his own spare bedroom. Move a chest of drawers and if you didn't put it back in precisely the same position you had a few nasty dents left to remind you what a fool you'd been. Evidently Mrs. S. had been suckered too. The chair was a good three inches back from where she usually kept it. Could mean nothing at all, of course, but on the other hand—drat it, there had to be a reason, though he couldn't see one. The plaster wall behind it was bare, with no furniture near enough to matter. Squeezing his considerable bulk between the chair and the fireside wall, he squinted down at the floor. It was in shadow, but his torch illuminated further marks which he examined closely before straightening up.

" I'll want these photographed. Something else has stood here. Any idea what?"

She racked her brain in vain. " I'm sorry, I can't remember."

" Small side-table? Whatnot? Stand of potted palms?"

" No plants of any kind, I'm sure of that." Kneeling on the brightly-patterned seat, she peered over the back of it and saw two small rectangular impressions about sixteen inches apart. The other two (if this was a four-legged object) were presumably hidden by the chair in its new position. She had to admit being baffled.

Lovick looked at his colleague. " Where's Smith?"

" Photographing the bedroom, sir."

" Tell him to pay extra attention to this corner."

" Yes, sir."

Miss Purdy said with a touch of distress : " You seem to be considering this business as murder."

" I'm taking no chances, especially since you mentioned an intruder. Anything else strike you?"

" Only that I wish he'd stolen her pictures."

" Pictures?" He looked round at the walls on which were hung half a dozen original oil-paintings, all of the kind he detested, and which he couldn't imagine anyone in his right mind wanting to give house-room to, let alone steal. " Why?"

" They're—obscene."

He walked over to one and looked at it more closely, wondering how you could pick out obscenity from the general mess which, in his opinion, was what all abstract painting amounted to. This lot looked as though some demented kid had spilt colours on the canvas and ridden a tricycle over them, though come to think of it—when you took a proper look—

He took a proper look and whistled softly. Hadn't struck him before but there *was* a kind of pattern to this one, a leering malicious face which peered through the lunatic kaleidoscope and seemed to follow you with its scummy eyes when you moved away. And the next—dammit, this one was downright pornographic, if it meant what he thought it did. No wonder Miss Purdy—

He said a little too loudly: " What about the bedroom?"

" I haven't seen it since she moved in."

" May as well take a look at it."

The bedroom opened, like the living-room, from a short narrow passage which ended at the kitchen door. Halfway along, the door of the broom-cupboard stood ajar and Miss Purdy stopped to look inside. For a woman uninterested in housework Mrs. Sibley had been well-equipped with tools but hadn't bothered much about looking after them. The bag of the vacuum-cleaner needed emptying, mop-head and dusters would have been better for a wash, a yellow plastic dustpan on the floor was in imminent danger of being crushed under the foot of a pair of steps, and a mess of dirty rags in a corner cried aloud for the nearest dustbin.

Lovick stopped too. " Anything important?"

" No, it seems to be in order. Mrs. Sibley's idea of order," she corrected herself with slight acidity. " Which isn't mine."

Women, thought Lovick, pushing the bedroom door wide

77

open. Murder, witchcraft, LSD or what-have-you, they still threw fits over fluff on the carpet. . . .

But it wasn't fluff on the carpet which brought Miss Purdy to a dead stop immediately inside the room. She didn't even see the carpet, let alone the fluff, and for all her mind registered of the furniture it could have been made of orange-boxes. Only one thing caught her attention, a small piece of wood-carving fixed to the wall above the bed-head, and its impact was so great that the room rocked round her and her throat-muscles refused to work. Never in her life had she been shaken by such an uprush of anger and revulsion.

She pointed a shaking finger at it and, after several ineffectual sounds, managed to make her meaning clear. " Get that out."

" Now look, Miss Purdy—"

" Get it out of my house."

" Sorry, I know how you feel, but—"

" *Get it out of my house.*"

Lovick looked at the photographer. " How much longer—"

" Just finished in here, sir."

" Then lift that thing off the wall and take it out to the car. Handle it carefully. It's evidence."

Evidence. . . . An inverted crucifix. . . . Miss Purdy swayed, clapped a hand to her mouth and plunged towards the bathroom. They heard her retching. . . .

When she came back a few minutes later, she looked white and shrunken but fully in command of herself. " Thank you, Inspector, it was kind of you to humour me. Now I'm going over to the church."

" Look, there are one or two more questions—"

" I'm sorry, they must wait. I'll go straight to your house afterwards. There—" she managed a wan smile—" you'll have me at your mercy."

" But you can't just hop off and—"

" I've no choice. I won't set foot in this house again until every stick of her furniture has been removed and the place has been exorcised."

CHAPTER SIX

After more than thirty years of marriage there was only one bone of contention between Lovick and his spry, energetic little wife, and that was Mrs. Lovick's hypochondriac sister who was for ever dragging her away to Birmingham and condemning him to a week or two of baked beans. Just now, however, the sister was coddling herself in a Torquay hydro and his missus was free to attend to her marital duties, which tonight meant steak-and-kidney pudding with mashed spuds and greens followed by apple-tart and cream.

Warmly invited to share this delectable feast, Miss Purdy declined gracefully and hoped her involuntary shudder didn't show. " It's very kind of you, Mrs. Lovick, but I've already had supper and I'm afraid I don't feel like more food at the moment. Perhaps a biscuit later on—"

" Baloney," said Lovick robustly. " Nothing like a good dollop of hot food inside to chase away the willies. I should know. The corpses I've come home from—"

" Albert !" said his wife.

" Eh? Oh, sorry. But biscuits ! There's horror if you like."

Nevertheless, a glass of sherry and a plain biscuit did make Miss Purdy feel better, though the real foundation for her improved peace of mind had been laid during her half-hour visit to the vicar of the church across the lane. Cleansed and fortified, she had secured his promise of a short service at the house tomorrow morning and now felt armoured against the living malevolence of a dead woman.

Lovick had spent the same half-hour flipping through the contents of Mrs. Sibley's bureau without much joy. Her bills and receipts were in reasonable order but he'd found precious little personal correspondence to go on, let alone anything to connect her with last night's fun and games at St. Edred's. Plenty of books on demonology and such on her shelves, and some of the illustrations would have scared the pants off most people, but either the intruder was unique or he'd needed his pants for something else—like carrying away letters or papers incriminating himself. Lovick had been able to find only one item of possible value. He pushed it across to Miss Purdy while awaiting his second helping of apple-tart.

" You didn't tell me your top flat's let again."

She stiffened alarmingly. " It isn't."

" Take a look at that, then."

' That ' was a letter addressed to Mrs. Sibley and post-marked Norwich, though the date was indecipherable. As Miss Purdy took out the carelessly-scrawled enclosure, her hackles were already rising, and by the time she reached the end of it her blood-pressure was up too. She had difficulty in finding adequate words.

' Dear Sibyl,' it ran. ' You and your smells, what a giggle, or do I mean spells? I always said you were an old witch and this proves it. We'll start packing right away. Sooner I get Zenna out of this rathole the better. How about moving in at the end of next week? Rent seems fair enough but no harm in trying to beat the old cow down. She didn't know what she was taking on when you breezed into her life! Can't quite see why you want us there but no grumbling from this side, we'll help all we can. Zenna hasn't stopped talking since we saw the flat, she's hooked on that view from the back window, already making curtains and—hold everything—gabbing about marriage. Me! Married! See what you've started? She'll end up voting Tory if we don't watch out. See you! Max.'

Miss Purdy's throat-muscles finally unknotted themselves. "Saw the flat, he says. What—how—when could they possibly have—"

"Don't worry, we'll ask him. Who is he?"

"Max?" She eyed the signature with loathing. "Her step-son, I suppose. She called him a writer, though if this is a sample of his style—" Another point hit her. "And this—this Zenna woman! Mrs. Sibley said they were already married."

"Had to, or you'd have hit the roof. Let's hear about the smells."

Her version was concise. Since he was her host, she refrained from pointing out that if he'd listened to her in the first place Mrs. Sibley might still be alive. That is, if he'd done something about it; the woman would hardly have risked attending a witches' sabbat with a police investigation going on. Just what he'd have been able to do about it was another matter. Witchcraft is no longer a crime, and short of finding tangible evidence of fraud or harassment—

Predictably, he waved every other possibility aside. "Of course she worked it! We'll pull the place apart tomorrow and if we can't find out how, I'll eat my boots."

"You rule out any form of spell, then?"

He choked on a mouthful of tart. "Look, if you're trying to sell me that kind of hokum—'

"Her step-son doesn't contradict it."

"He was joking."

"A remarkably apt joke, under the circumstances."

Scooping up the last spoonful of apple and cream, he pushed his plate aside and pulled out his pipe, giving an elaborate impression of patience. "Suppose you take your blinkers off and look at facts. She may or may not have imagined she could ride on a broomstick, right?"

"Well—"

"And if she tried she fell off, so she was a pretty duff witch at best. And if she couldn't stay on a simple broomstick, am I supposed to believe she created a stink upstairs by cavorting in the nude on the marshes and screeching silly incantations? Be your age."

Miss Purdy was nettled. "There's more to it than that. Even if most so-called witchcraft can be put down to the power of suggestion, there's a hard core of downright evil left, with power of its own, and some people are wicked enough to tap that power."

"Oh, for Pete's sake!" He flung up his hands, nearly knocking over the coffee his wife was about to set in front of him. "She was a stupid cantankerous old woman hellbent on getting that top flat for her relations and it's all England to a bag of doughnuts I'll find some sort of stink-bomb up there, so forget spells and stick to common sense. What about her background?"

"I've told you all I know. Her late husband—"

"Hardware in the Midlands, I've got that bit. Any kids?"

"Only this step-son, as far as I know."

"He'll probably inherit, then."

"You must ask Mr. Begbie about that."

"Oh yes, her solicitor. What about her other pals in Wrexley?"

"She belonged to the Antiquarian Society."

"Wetherby and Dillinger and that lot?"

"They're both members, certainly. So are Mr. Begbie and Major Barlow and a number of other respectable people. I'd say her best friend was Miss Turnberry, though I'm not sure about the quality of the friendship. From what Margery Daw told me—"

"Margery *who*?"

83

"Margery Daw, Miss Turnberry's niece. She didn't like the way Mrs. Sibley domineered over her aunt. As for Miss Turnberry herself, I'm bound to admit her anxiety today struck me as excessive. Not bogus exactly, but—well, unhealthy, though I'm probably doing her an injustice. Her personality is slightly unbalanced at the best of times. How did she take the news of Mrs. Sibley's death?"

"Hysterics. A woman cop's staying the night with her." But Lovick wasn't interested in Miss Turnberry. "This Margery Daw—any relation to Kenneth Daw?"

"His wife. They live at Witchwater. I daresay you know the cottage has been rebuilt."

"I do now." His tone was grim. "Met young Daw this morning and made a few enquiries afterwards. Begbie unearthed him, I understand, and Dillinger built the cottage. Funny how your Antiquarians keep turning up."

"You know Mrs. Sibley put up most of the money?"

"If that's supposed to make it respectable—"

"It isn't, but you can't tar everybody with the same brush. Their interest wasn't necessarily the same as hers, though I agree the business needs investigating. In my opinion, the most sinister contribution she made was to provide a cat."

"For Pete's sake! What's wrong with—"

"A big black vicious cat that wears a silver collar and goes by the name of—"

"Elimauzer!" His fist thumped down on the table with a vigour that rattled his empty cup and reached his wife's ears in the kitchen. "And now tell me it's the ghost of that one we shot a few years back—"

"It isn't, but it's a definite attempt to resurrect him."

He was saved from choking by the ringing of the phone.

When he came back from answering it, his expression was bleakly official. "Suzi Barlow," he said tersely. "When did you see her last?"

" I had tea with her this afternoon in Norwich."

" What's she like?"

" A little odd, perhaps. Not a good reputation. But a very pretty girl who—"

" Not any longer. She's dead."

" Dead!"

" Ken Daw has just found her on the marshes with ruddy great cat-scratches on her cheek." He swung round and made for the door again, calling to his wife over his shoulder. " Don't wait up for me, Sarah! This looks like taking all night."

* * *

By the light of arc-lamps as well as a full moon, Lovick looked down at his second corpse within five hours, his view slightly impeded by a ground-mist which, though not very thick just here, managed nevertheless to convey the macabre effect of a semi-transparent shroud.

In life Suzi Barlow had undoubtedly been beautiful. In death, sprawling half in and half out of the narrow uncleared dyke into which she'd apparently fallen in head-long flight, she was not. Her face showed an expression of appalling terror. One leg was crumpled under her while the other, dragging helplessly in water, was given a grotesque illusion of life by the sinuous movement of underwater weeds in the sluggish curent. Both arms were upflung, still clutching the dead reeds fringing the dyke— and if ever you needed an illustration of what a broken reed was like to cling to, he thought grimly, this was it.

And those scratches—

The devil of it was he'd been through all this before. Different corpse, different time of year, but otherwise a dead ringer for another part of the Jessica Daw murder. That other poor woman—what was her name? Jo Anderson—had died in this same dyke in the depths of winter when the surrounding marshes had been frozen solid and every tuft of coarse grass and clump of dead stems had been white with rime; when the stiff brown reeds had been rooted in broken ice and the east wind tearing across the arctic waste had been vicious enough to freeze his bones. And *she* hadn't looked pretty either, what with her cheek scratched to ribbons and—

He swore aloud.

That blasted cat.

Not the same cat, of course. With his own eyes he'd seen the original beast shot. But its twin brother, apparently. And if Miss Purdy wasn't dreaming some fool or lunatic had given it the same hellish name, Elimauzer, which came straight out of some blessed mediaeval book about witch-finders, the name of a witch's familiar or some such rubbish. And the duplication had been deliberate, even to the extent of shoving a silver collar round its neck. The *same* collar, presumably, which had been Daw property for generations according to Jessica and which had probably been handed over to Begbie in trust for her heirs, if any. And now the heir had been dug up, the cottage rebuilt, another Elimauzer was on the prowl and another woman had died running away from him in terror. . . .

The police-surgeon came over to join him, harsh shadows cast on his face by the conflict of natural and unnatural lighting. " Well, there you are, Lovick. No knowing what the post-mortem will turn up but I can't find any other cause of death at this stage. Leg broken and she couldn't get out of the dyke, that's obvious, though I'd have thought a young and healthy woman—damn it all, she can't have been lying there more than a couple of hours. Should have thought she'd be able to last that long."

" With a cat ravaging around?"

The doctor's shoulders hunched and dropped again.

"Weak heart, maybe. You know she's an addict?"

"Was, is my information."

"Like to bet? Ah, the ambulance men. Okay to take her away?"

"She's all yours."

The cameraman had already taken pictures of the body, but though Sergeant Stebbings and P.C. Cocker, on Lovick's instructions, were casting round for anything they might find, a proper search would have to wait till daylight. And a fat chance of any evidence turning up, thought Lovick sourly, turning to survey the one person they knew had arrived on the scene before them, the man who'd given the alarm, the missing heir in person, the owner of that blasted cat and a blood relative of the witch-girl who'd died six years ago. . . .

Well, these spring nights were damned cold and the grass was wet. Blessed if he was going to stand out here any longer risking rheumatism. Only one question was vital now.

He put it brusquely. "Where's that bloody cat?"

Guarded by P.C. Saunders, Kenneth Daw had been giving a good imitation of a stone statue. Now he looked at Lovick as though he'd never seen him before. It was a full ten seconds before his lips moved.

"Is she—dead?"

"You knew that before you called me."

"I—I hoped—" His mouth worked. "The cat? I don't know. Gone home, I suppose. She—Suzi—was scared of cats."

"Not the only one, if the cat's called Elimauzer and wears a silver collar."

"That wasn't my doing."

"Your wife's, then?"

"No, she—she—" Suddenly his eyes widened, focusing on a spot beyond the searchers. An oath escaped him and

87

he came violently to life. " Margery! What the hell—"

At first it seemed like the old trick of diversion, especially when he immediately plunged away in a different direction altogether, evading Saunders with a lightning twist and leaping over the dyke to vanish in the mist at a crouching run. But Lovick, startled into turning, had caught a quick glimpse of a woman hovering some distance away, her white face swimming in the hazy moonlight, and his galvanising shout scattered pursuers in both directions.

" After them, you fools!"

The girl would be easily caught, she was making for Witchwater and Cocker had once had visions of an Olympic gold, but Ken Daw was a different matter; he'd had the wit to keep his head below mist-level and where he was heading now was anybody's guess. Nowhere out there to head to, anyway. Why in Pete's name he'd bolted—

Lovick swore again. " This Margery—"

" His wife, sir," said the cameraman, busy packing up his gear.

" I guessed that, nitwit, I'm not daft. What I meant—" He broke off, straining his eyes. Difficult to be sure but it looked as though the capture had already taken place. He grunted when Cocker returned shortly afterwards holding her by the arm. She was shivering as well as crying, not surprising seeing the young ninny had come out in a thin jumper and slacks, not even a cardigan at this time of night. How silly could you get?

He said austerely: " What do you think you're playing at?"

" I—I—where's Ken?"

" Hopped it."

She fired up a little. " If you've been frightening him—"

" Heaven give me patience. What do you know about tonight's business?"

" Nothing, except—" her lips shook—" except the cat

got loose and—and Ken rushed out to find it and—and I—I waited and waited and he didn't come back, so I thought I'd better go out and help him look."

"Where is it now?"

"I don't know." The noise that escaped her was something between a snuffle and a sob. And then her head lifted. "And w-what's more, I don't care, I hope I never see it again. I used to *like* cats, but that one—it's mean and vicious and—"

"Why do you keep it if—"

"We have to, it's in the agreement."

"What agreement? Oh, to heck with it. We'll do this in the warm." Turning, he gave Stebbings rapid instructions. The stretcher-bearers had already taken their covered burden to the ambulance waiting in the lane where the police cars had been left, and the doctor too had gone. No sign yet of Ken or Saunders. He cast a frowning glance in the direction of Witchwater but decided against traipsing over there to talk. He'd done enough walking lately. This interview would take place at the nick.

"This way," he said abruptly, taking her by the elbow. She hung back, frightened. "You can't arrest me, I haven't done anything."

"Nobody said you had."

"I've got to get home. I left the door wide open and the kettle on."

"In a hurry, weren't you?"

"I didn't expect to be out long."

"Never mind, Cocker will keep an eye on things." He spoke briefly to the young constable, who saluted and turned to retrace his footsteps towards Witchwater, concealing whatever feelings he had at the prospect of meeting Elimauzer.

Lovick turned back to Margery. "Now, young lady—"

He guided her towards the car, following the cattle-track

89

leading to Pizey's Cottage and the lane.

In his own room at the station, both bars of the electric fire on and his pipe drawing comfortably, he mellowed inwardly as well as outwardly. Margery, too, looked better after a cup of tea from the canteen and he eyed her with something approaching benevolence. Pretty kid, nice open face, straight fair hair and a freckle or two—looked as though the last of the Daws had struck lucky. Not much colour in her cheeks at the moment but more than she'd had in that spook-ridden moonlight. Thinking which, he proceeded to take it away again.

"You know what Ken found in the dyke?"

Her face grew paper-white. "Somebody—fell in—"

"He told you so?"

"No, I never spoke to him on the marshes, I never got nearer than where you saw me. I'd just got there when——"

"Then how did you know there'd been an accident?"

"The lights—and all you cops—and the men taking her away——"

He pounced on that. "Her?"

A sudden spark of hope lit her eyes. "Wasn't it?"

"I'm asking how you knew it."

She sagged back. "I—I thought he'd gone out to meet a girl."

"What girl?"

"Do I have to answer that?"

"Not unless you want to, but——" Compunction struck him. "Look, if you're too tired—or if a lawyer would help——"

She said listlessly: "I used to work for Mr. Begbie."

Ah yes, Miss Purdy had mentioned that, and hadn't she also said she knew the girl? A policewoman was in the room as a matter of form, but it wasn't a policewoman the kid needed, it was a friend. So if Miss Purdy hadn't gone to bed—

90

A quick phone call reassured him and, pleased with this proof of his own benevolence, he replaced the receiver. "Miss Purdy's coming round to hold your hand. Okay?"

Margery smiled for the first time since he'd met her. Sending out for fresh tea he leaned back in his chair, drumming softly on the desk with his fingers and waiting.

Miss Purdy arrived in less than five minutes, just in time for the tea to draw. Though still pale herself, her smile was warm and friendly as she pulled up a chair close to the girl and took her hand. "My dear, I know very little of what this is about but I'm here to help you, so if the inspector will be kind enough to put me in the picture—" She looked at him enquiringly.

"Nothing for Mrs. Daw to be afraid of. Her husband found the body and then scarpered. Nothing against him whatever—so far—and the sooner he turns up again the sooner we can all go home to bed. Meanwhile, Mrs. Daw was on the scene too—within a hundred yards or so, anyway—so I think you'll agree I'm entitled to know what she was doing there."

"You're not accusing her of participation?"

"I'm not accusing her of anything. I'm not accusing anybody of anything," said Lovick, his benevolence rapidly changing to exasperation. "I'm ruddy well leaning over backwards to avoid accusing anything in creation except that perishing cat."

"This isn't a case of murder?"

"Not as far as I know. Way it looks at present, the girl was running away from the cat, broke her leg in the dyke and couldn't get out. May have been complications like a weak heart, but—"

Miss Purdy said bleakly: "She hated cats."

"So young Daw told me."

"I was right, then," said Margery suddenly. "It was Suzi Barlow."

" You knew she was on the marshes?"

" No, but—" She stopped. Her cup went down with a clatter. " You said—body—"

" Yes. She's dead."

Without a sound the girl slumped back in her chair.

CHAPTER SEVEN

Passing smelling-salts under Margery's nose, Miss Purdy told Lovick with some acerbity that he should take lessons on how to break bad news.

Stung, Lovick demanded how the heck he was supposed to know the two girls were anything but strangers. "And rivals at that. You heard what she said. Daw went out to meet the Barlow wench and—"

"She didn't say that."

"She did to me, before you came. At least, she said he'd gone out to meet a girl, and all I did was provide the ruddy name. And what's more—" He broke off. "All right, you can stop waving that thing about. She's coming round."

"You know she's pregnant?"

He flung up his hands. "And now you tell me! Am I supposed to have second sight?"

"You're supposed to have common sense at least. She's in no state to answer any more questions."

In point of fact, Margery hadn't lost consciousness completely. The room had begun to spin and their voices had receded to an immeasurable distance, reaching her as sounds without meaning, part of an inescapable nightmare. Now, however, things were coming back into focus and she made an effort to sit up, blindly pushing away the hand with the smelling-salts. " I—want—Ken—"

"He'll be here soon, dear," said Miss Purdy comfortingly.

"He hasn't done anything wrong."

"Of course not."

"We couldn't help the cat getting out."

"Don't talk about it, don't even think about it. Would you like to go home?"

But this well-meant suggestion brought a reaction of sheer terror. "No! No! Not without Ken. He'll be here— you promised—"

"No need to go anywhere if you don't want to. We'll wait for him here. And now, my dear, your tea—"

"Try a spot of this," said Lovick gruffly, adding a thimbleful of brandy from his own flask.

Responding gratefully to the changed atmosphere, Margery sipped her tea and, after a few minutes, said with a brave imitation of normality: "I'm all right now, and I don't mind answering questions. Honest, I'd like to, Inspector, then you won't have to bother Ken so much. What do you want to know?"

"If you're sure—"

"We've got nothing to hide, either of us."

"Good." He glanced briefly at the policewoman in the corner, who at once took out her notebook and began to make unobtrusive notes. "First of all, Mrs. Daw, what can you tell me about Suzi Barlow?"

Her eyes clouded but there was no hesitation. "Not much because I never met her, Inspector, though of course I've heard a lot about her, who hasn't? I mean, coming down from London and all those tales flying about—"

"Did she mind gossip?"

"Not from what Ken told me—he works for the major, you know. Brazen, he called her—decadent—I think that's the word. He's a bit funny in some ways, doesn't go for drugs and pop-stars, says it's all part of this rotten Establishment and we won't get right till we've blown ourselves up. But lately—well, I got this feeling—he still said she wasn't his type and I believed him until—" She stopped, casting a desperate glance at Miss Purdy.

" Until last night?" prompted Miss Purdy gently.

" That's right, it was just too bad of her to make him fly her all that way without notice and not getting home till two in the morning, and me with no phone or anything and the baby coming, he *knows* how I hate being in that place alone at night. Well, I suppose it wasn't his fault really, but I do think——"

" Just a minute," interrupted Lovick, suddenly alert. " You're talking about last night?"

She nodded vigorously. Anger had brought a sparkle to her eyes and fresh colour to her cheeks. " And all to see this silly pop-star, Ricky Rainbow, would you believe it? Ken said he hadn't any choice, he had to carry out orders, but there is a limit and I said——"

" They went in the helicopter?"

" That's what I'm telling you, isn't it? She did lend him her car to get back as far as Wrexley, but——"

" Last night," said Lovick, spacing the words precisely, " there was monkey-business at St. Edred's. What do you know about that?"

" St. Edred's?" She stared at him. " You mean those ruins over towards Bilby?"

" Oh, so you've heard of them."

" Everybody's heard of them, I used to play there when I was a kid. But—monkey-business—what sort of——"

" Both Major Barlow and his grand-daughter denied the chopper was taken out."

" But—but Ken said——"

He turned on Miss Purdy. " You knew about this pop-star trip and didn't tell me?"

She was genuinely upset. " Believe me, Inspector, I've only just seen the implications."

" *What* implications?" Margery's voice rose on a note of incipient hysteria. " You sit there talking about things I've never heard of—what's St. Edred's got to do with them going off to Newmarket?"

"Newmarket?" Lovick reached for the phone. "Is that where this pop-star lives?"

"Near there, anyway, he's got a big house and some stables, I don't know the exact address. He runs race-horses as well as—"

"What's his name again?"

"Ricky Rainbow. But—"

"I'll bet." Dialling, he got through to the Newmarket police, waving her to silence when she started to speak again.

After a brief conversation he hung up.

"Known there all right. Real name Charles Higgins. They'll ring back after getting his version of last night, which I sincerely hope tallies with your husband's, Mrs. Daw, though I must warn you I have my doubts."

"You think—Ken was lying too?"

"Somebody was, and if only the young fool hadn't bolted—" His ears cocked at the sound of raised voices outside. "Ah! He seems to have arrived."

She tensed, sitting bolt upright watching the door. Ken's voice came through clearly. "Where is she? You've got no bloody right—"

Miss Purdy laid a warning hand on her arm. Lovick said smoothly: "Don't worry, Mrs. Daw, we've nothing against him at present. Far as I know, he's simply the bloke who found Suzi Barlow's body, and all I'm asking is a bit of help."

*　　*　　*

It wasn't all he intended to ask by a long way, especially after seeing P.C. Saunders' dripping uniform and rapidly-blooming shiner, but Margery got in first. Throwing all minor matters overboard she jumped up with an anguished

96

cry. "Ken! Your lip! What's happened to your lip?"

He dashed away a trickle of blood. " I'm all right, dammit, but you——"

"Oh, Ken! It's been so awful!" She collapsed in his arms, hiccupping with sobs. " I never meant all those things I said, and when you ran away I thought——I thought——"

"Shut up!" He held her close but his tone was almost savage. His tormented eyes looked across at Lovick. "Haven't you any heart? She ought to be at home in bed, not——"

"Miss Purdy can take her to another room."

"No!" Margery's head jerked up. "You'd only start bullying him and——"

"Oh, for Pete's sake! Do you think I'm doing this for fun? If you want to stay, sit down and be quiet."

Ken himself pushed her back into her chair, giving Miss Purdy a hard stare as he did so. Miss Purdy returned it with interest. Oddly, despite his haggard mud-streaked face and the cut and swollen lip, she liked what she saw, feeling instinctively he was on the right side of the fence. Lovick, remembering the stiff self-contained young pilot who'd given him a lift over the marshes this morning, reflected with satisfaction that he'd lost some of his stuffing, but soon found that Ken was very far from being defeated. Careless of what anyone thought of him, he swung back to face the desk.

"Look, this has nothing to do with Margery and she's three months gone with a baby. Leave her out of it, do you hear? Otherwise I'll sue you for——"

"Don't be a young idiot," said Lovick, exasperated. " If you hadn't scarpered we'd all be in bed by now, so shut up and don't interrupt. Saunders?"

P.C. Saunders, more conscious of sodden trouser-legs than anything else, wrenched his mind away from visions of permanent rheumatism and tried to concentrate on his report. " Lost him in the mist, sir, but I reckoned he'd be doubling back home and I was right. Found him at Witchwater just climbing into his boat. We had a bit of a scuffle on the bank—"

" In the water too, by the look of it."

" Yes, sir, but after I said his wife was at the station he couldn't get here quick enough, no trouble at all bar a bit of bad language. We came by water," he added with a touch of envy. " Nice little boat. Didn't take more than ten minutes."

" I'm not interested in boats." Lovick leaned back in his chair, eyeing Ken without noticeable affection. " I want to know why young Daw bolted."

" Why shouldn't I?" asked Ken belligerently. " I hadn't done anything wrong."

" Then why did you?"

" Because—" He gave in suddenly. " Okay, I hoped you'd come after me and leave her alone."

" Why were you on the marshes in the first place?"

" No law against taking a walk."

" No sense in it either, far as I can see, unless you went to meet Suzi Barlow."

" I didn't know she'd be—"

" Don't give me that. Even your wife doesn't believe it."

Margery was on her feet at once. " I didn't say that. I said I only *thought*—"

" Why the hell couldn't you keep your mouth shut?" Ken shouted at her. " You might have known everything would get twisted. If only you'd stayed at home—"

" I was frightened, couldn't you see that? The way you looked when you dashed out—"

" I dashed out to find that blasted cat."

" Which you wouldn't have done," cut in Lovick

98

pointedly, " except for somebody who was scared of cats."

Ken swore vividly. " All right, I did go out to meet her, but not for the reason you all think. I wasn't in love with her or anything like that. I haven't seen her all day, she's been in Norwich at some lecture or other and I left the Hall before she got back. But when I dropped in at the pub—"

" Which pub?"

" My usual. The ' Blue Lion ' at Felling. Landlord called me to the phone and it was Suzi, she said she'd got to speak to me urgently."

" What about?"

" She wouldn't say over the phone. Told me to meet her halfway between Witchwater and Pizey's at eleven o'clock. She couldn't make it earlier because of her grandfather."

" What time was this phone call?"

" Early. Not much after seven. I don't stay out late because of Margery."

" Why didn't you tell me she'd called?" demanded his wife fiercely. " Sitting there eating your supper and never a word about going out later—"

" You'd have hit the roof. This bee you've got about her—"

" It's more than a bee. Look at last night, keeping you out to all hours. How do I know you weren't smooching with her instead of—"

" I tell you, it doesn't mean a thing, I didn't want to worry you, that's all. If you hadn't let that ruddy cat out—"

" *I* let it out! Why, it was you who opened the door and—"

" And you who kept me arguing till—"

" That's enough," said Lovick with authority. " I've got the picture. Did you see the cat, Daw?"

" No."

" Or speak to Suzi Barlow?"

" No, damn you. No!"

" All right. How long before you found her?"

" About—twenty minutes." There were beads of sweat on his forehead.

" Was she still alive?"

" No."

" You're sure of that?"

" As sure as anyone can be. I had a torch and as soon as I saw those scratches—" His eyes closed for a moment. " If you must know, I was sick. I thought of going home and saying nothing but—I couldn't leave her out there all night. So I rang from Pizey's—our nearest phone—and waited there till your sergeant came."

" Did you see the cat at any time?"

" No, but—in that mist—"

" And you've no idea what she wanted to see you about?"

" I told you, she wouldn't say."

" Where did you go in the chopper last night?"

Ken's eyes were stony. " Newmarket."

" Not St. Edred's, by any chance?"

" No."

Lovick regarded him levelly for several seconds and then switched points. " And now tell me where you were going in that boat."

*   *   *

Half an hour later he let them go.

Ken had sworn there'd been no intention of flight. The shock of Suzi's death had knocked him sideways and all he'd wanted was a quiet spot in which to hole up for an hour or two while sorting things out in his mind, getting ready to face a barrage of questions from his wife as well as the police.

" He'd had a shock all right," Lovick commented to Miss Purdy the following morning over breakfast. " I'm wondering how much of it was due to guilty conscience."

Miss Purdy pushed back her plate of half-eaten toast. " Just what are you suggesting, Inspector? That he had a hand in her death?"

" I'm suggesting there's more to it than he let on. He had a shock, right? He also had a nervous, pregnant wife who needed comforting more than he did. Would anyone with a clear conscience have kept her dangling for a couple of hours while he sat in a boat and communed with the moorhens? He was afraid to face her, that's what, which means there was a sight more to his relationship with Suzi Barlow than he'd like her to know about."

Miss Purdy said slowly : " It's his wife he's in love with. He proved that by coming to her rescue at the station."

" Rescue be damned, minute he knew we'd got her he couldn't reach us fast enough to shut her mouth. So what was he afraid she'd tell us?"

" Well, what?"

" This Newmarket yarn. They'd cooked it up to account for his being home late that night. Strictly for home consumption. But after Mrs. Sibley's death the Barlow girl panicked and swore the chopper hadn't been out at all, so she had to see him before the police did and get him to back her up, his wife too if necessary. Unfortunately for young Daw—"

" She'd already passed the Newmarket story on to me."

" Exactly. So he was stymied. The point is, did he tell Suzi so before she died or—"

" She was already dead when—"

" So he *said*. But if the cat had a silver collar, it presumably had a lead. What was to stop him catching the beast first and loosing it at her afterwards?"

Miss Purdy's back stiffened. "Can you suggest a motive?"

"Easily. He had more to lose than she had if it came out they'd been at St. Edred's. She didn't give a damn what people thought of her, but he has a wife. She could have broken up their marriage without even trying."

"I don't believe he's capable of——"

"Don't you? The Newmarket alibi's busted anyway. Word came through half an hour ago. Ricky Rainbow—alias Charlie Higgins—hasn't set eyes on Suzi Barlow for at least three months."

* * *

A simple form of exorcism took place at Miss Purdy's house an hour later. The focus of evil was the dead woman's bedroom. The vicar flinched visibly on the threshold before entering and it took all Miss Purdy's courage to follow him inside, where the malevolence gathering to oppose them was all but palpable. But though his voice faltered more than once, the hand holding aloft the cross remained steady, and suddenly there was——

How could one describe it? Not a wind, the window was shut. Not a cry, there was no sound. Not a visible change, the room looked exactly as it had done a moment before. And yet——

And yet something had gone. Gone unwillingly and with a violence of hatred that left the onlookers shaken, but—gone, and in its place was the blessing of indescribable peace.

Miss Purdy remained on her knees for a long while after the priest had left, . . .

Brisk and practical, she had no intention of leaving it at that. Spiritually the house was cleansed, physically the whole of that flat must be stripped and redecorated with the least possible delay, leaving not so much as a fingerprint of its late occupant behind. Every item of Mrs. Sibley's furniture would go into store the moment Lovick gave permission, whether the step-son had turned up or not. Only then, she felt, could she really write ' finis ' to the most unsavoury experience of her life.

Dillinger or Breck? Either would probably carry out her instructions adequately, but she didn't hesitate a moment before deciding on Breck. However incompetent or unlucky with his other jobs, he'd done his best to cope with the very odd problems upstairs and she didn't think it was his fault he hadn't succeeded. His account of the break-up between himself and Dillinger might or might not be accurate, but that wasn't the point. Set one against the other—dour bluntness against jovial expansiveness—and she found she preferred the bluntness.

Remembering Dillinger's heavily-playful passes at Suzi in Norwich yesterday, she wondered how he was taking the news of her death. If he'd had hopes of making her the second Mrs. Dillinger, it looked as though the Midas touch had deserted him, though she rather doubted his chances anyway. Especially with a good-looking boy like Kenneth Daw in the offing.

She caught that thought back sharply. Whatever else was in doubt, she was quite sure Ken loved his wife. Suzi's wiles might have knocked him off balance temporarily—though there was no proof even of that—but a serious attempt to hook him wouldn't have stood a chance. Yet if Dillinger had thought otherwise—

Her mind went sliding on in spite of herself, picturing him following ' his ' girl on to the marshes, watching the meeting between her and Ken, grabbing Elimauzer by the collar, loosing him when—

Nonsense. She wasn't writing fiction now.

Picking up the phone, she dialled Breck's number. " Miss

103

Purdy here. Can you manage another job before you leave Wrexley? I want the middle flat entirely redecorated."

"I thought Dillinger—"

"I want it done again."

There was a brief pause. "It'll have to be pretty soon."

"It can't be too soon for me. Will you come and see it for yourself?"

"Right away, ma'am."

He was there inside fifteen minutes. News of Mrs. Sibley's bizarre death and the 'goings-on' at St. Edred's were already flying round the town and he warned her with grim satisfaction that she'd best keep an eye open for reporters.

"Looks as though I was right, don't it? Calling her an old witch. Her and her pal Dillinger—" He made a mime of spitting. "I reckon it was them as jinxed me. Maybe things'll be a bit cleaner from now on."

"You've no right to bring Mr. Dillinger into it."

"Ha'n't I? All right, ma'am, we'll see."

He didn't seem to have heard of Suzi's death, for which she was thankful. Leading the way upstairs she reverted to business. "You understand, Mr. Breck, I can't give you an exact starting date until the police have finished with the flat, but Inspector Lovick has promised it won't be long."

"Suits me, ma'am, I'm in two minds about leavin' now. Thought I'd wait a while and see how the wind blows. Complete re-decoration you said?"

"The more complete the better."

She had no qualms now about entering the flat. P.C. Saunders was on duty inside the living-room, going through the contents of the desk. He started to get up but she shook her head.

"Don't let us disturb you. This is simply a tour of inspection."

Breck absorbed the garish, expensive decor with sour distaste. "Can't blame you for wanting it changed, ma'am. Sets your teeth on edge, don't it? What colour will you have the walls?"

"Plain white. And a new brick fireplace instead of those hideous tiles. And that dreadful polystyrene ceiling will have to go." She looked up at the square segments with repugnance. "I can't imagine why she bothered, the original plaster is perfectly sound. It completely spoils the proportions of the room."

"And I wouldn't call it properly put up neither." He pointed to the far corner where a couple of the twelve-inch squares were slightly out of true. "And they say it's me that's incompetent! Beats me how Dillinger's lasted so long, let alone growing fat on it."

Miss Purdy was getting rather tired of his preoccupation with Dillinger, but in this case he had a point. Those tiles shouldn't have dropped in the short time since they'd been put up. It was the same corner in which the armchair had been pushed too far back, leaving its former imprints on the carpet. The imprints were still clearly visible, and remembering the other indentations in the space behind it she again tried to visualise a potted palm or whatnot standing there and failed. Mrs. Sibley herself had been sitting in that chair on the one occasion when she'd been asked inside and surely the background could hardly have failed to register if—

Suddenly two things clicked together and became one. The out-of-true tiles above and—in the passage outside—

"Steps!" she said aloud.

Breck stared at her and the constable looked up alertly.

"A pair of wooden steps!" she repeated with rising excitement. "In the broom-cupboard outside. Has anyone thought to compare its feet with the marks behind this chair, Saunders?"

105

Saunders got to his feet. " I wouldn't know, ma'am, having only just come on duty, but if you're thinking of moving anything—"

" Oh, don't be silly, it's my house after all and I'll take full responsibility. I should have thought of this last night." As she spoke she was hurrying out into the passage and pulling open the cupboard door. " Palm-stand, indeed! No palm-stand ever—ah, here we are!" Seizing the lightweight wooden steps, she upended them and pointed in triumph to the base of the feet. " Exactly the right size and shape! I'm positive they'll match up."

" What are you going to do with them?" asked Saunders in alarm.

" Try them, of course. And if I'm right—"

" Mrs. Sibley stood on 'em to reach those tiles!" exclaimed Breck, suddenly enlightened.

" Mrs. Sibley—or an intruder I heard yesterday morning."

" Ah, that's more like! If he was in a hurry and didn't stop to put 'em back properly—"

" At least it's worth investigating."

" Now see here, ma'am," began the harassed constable. " You can't go shifting—"

" But this is vital! It may be connected with what's been happening in the top flat. Ring Inspector Lovick if you must, but I'm sure he won't object—" Being truthful by nature she chopped that short, fully aware that he'd not only object to her taking matters into her own hands but would make no bones about saying so. She looked at Breck, determined not to be baulked of her fun. " I'd say we're on the verge of laying a ghost, wouldn't you?"

" By gosh, ma'am!" he said explosively. " You've said it!"

CHAPTER EIGHT

Steps and imprints matched exactly.

In the first glow of excitement Miss Purdy lost her head, pushed Saunders out of the way and held the steps steady while Breck climbed high enough to stretch up and run his fingers along the slightly-displaced rim of the nearest tile. There was a small click and both tiles swung downwards together, unified by plywood backing hinged on to a wooden slat. The plaster behind them had been cut away and the dim outline of beams loomed in the cavity.

" See that, ma'am?" Breck was more animated than she'd ever seen him. " Them's the joists of—"

" The top bedroom," she supplied after rapidly visualising the layout.

" And there's my wires for the central heating. Going along—for the love of—wait a minute!" His voice rose in uncontrollable excitement. " Well, I'm blowed! Of all the bloody—got a torch, ma'am?"

Meanwhile Saunders was frantically trying to phone Lovick, handicapped by the fact that he couldn't very well pull in one of his superior's best friends for obstruction. Normally Miss Purdy would never have dreamed of taking advantage of this fact, but she'd been through a lot lately. The troubles in the top flat had definitely unsettled if not demoralised her, and the prospect of finding an immediate and reasonable solution was too heady to be ignored.

No torch being handy, she switched on a table-lamp and passed it up to him, first discarding the shade. " Will this do?"

Holding it into the cavity as far as the flex would allow, Breck craned his neck to examine the spidery spaces under the top floorboards. Almost immediately an expletive broke from him. "Dillinger! I'd know his work anywhere. He's a good electrician, I'll say that for him, but what he reckoned he was up to—"

Saunders slammed the receiver down. "That's enough! Come down at once! Inspector's on his way and flaming mad by the sound of him. As much as my skin's worth to let this go on."

Miss Purdy came to her senses. "You're right, of course, it was unforgivable of me to allow it. Please come down, Mr. Breck. We're tampering with evidence."

"But look—this master-switch—"

"It must wait for Inspector Lovick."

Full of his find, Breck came down reluctantly. "A master-switch, see? Fixed to the next joist. I'll swear it wasn't there when I had them floorboards up. He's mucked about up there since those kids started complainin'—an' that's another thing I saw, ma'am, a length o' tubing fixed to some sort o' plastic container, an' you want to bet what's in it? Your damned smell, that's what. Look up, an' you can see daylight, not just a crack in the floorboards but a proper hole to take the nozzle o' that tubing—mebbe under their wardrobe or something. All she had to do was shove the tube through the hole and squeeze the container. Ghosts!" He spat into the fireplace. "That switch has been plugged into my system, see? Turn it off and you'd think the heating was still on upstairs only of course it wouldn't be, you'd be lying there shivering. And then with the smell hitting you as well—"

"I hope to goodness you haven't destroyed any fingerprints," said Miss Purdy from the bottom of her heart.

"What's it matter? We know who done it. Dillinger put that ceiling up, didn't he? So he must ha' known what that

108

corner was going to be used for."

"We can't prove it without fingerprints."

"Oh, can't we, though!" He gave a sudden chuckle. "Summat else up besides fingerprints, he's left one o' his tools behind. Spotted it just as you called me down, and I'll lay it's got his initials on. We allers used to cut our initials, saves grabbing the other fellow's tools and you don't drop habits like that. Your inspector's only got to take one look—"

"Mr. Breck, there's a law of slander."

"You tryin' to stand up for him?"

"No, but there's no proof—"

"All the proof I want, ma'am. Plain as a pikestaff him and this witch were in cahoots. Wouldn't put it past him to ha' been one o' that lot cavortin' at St. Edred's t'other night. Why, it could ha' been him that shut her mouth. If she threatened to start talkin'—"

"You've no grounds for saying that."

"Mebbe not, but him being so *respectable* these days—" He spat the word out as though naming a crime. "He wouldn't like Miss Barlow, for one, knowin' he was runnin' about the marsh naked. Especially with an old crow like this 'un. More I think about it—"

"Will you stop and think properly for a moment? She couldn't have ruined him without exposing herself too."

"She didn't get a chance when she was dead. Or mebbe there was some other reason—like puttin' a spell on Miss Barlow—" All at once his face closed into granite. Only his eyes were alive. He stared at Miss Purdy for a long moment without speaking. At last he said, very slowly: "Mebbe—that's—what she's been doin' all along. Puttin' spells on folks, sometimes to oblige him an' sometimes not."

"If you're thinking of yourself—"

"I said there was a jinx on me, didn't I? Mebbe it was her doin' that new road went through. Mebbe it was her as knocked Billy Abel off that ladder. An' the wall that fell down—"

"Mr. Breck, you're talking nonsense."

"Am I? Am I?" Suddenly and shockingly he came to life again. "We'll see what Mr. Ruddy Dillinger has to say about it."

She caught at his sleeve as he tried to push past. "Mr. Breck! You can't—"

"Try an' stop me. All these months—" His mouth worked. "Me an' the missus—drivin' us crazy—" He jerked away. "You keep out of it. It's him an' me now, man to man, an' no flamin' witch to run to. I'll choke the truth out o' him if it's the last thing I ever—"

"You'll stay here." Lovick's bulky, authoritative figure blocked the doorway. "Nobody's going anywhere till I say so." His face grew slightly purple as a sweeping glance took in the steps in the corner and the opening above. "Saunders! I'll have something to say to you later. Meanwhile—"

Miss Purdy turned pink. "It's not the constable's fault, Inspector, I take full responsibility. It suddenly occurred to me that those indentations on the carpet matched—"

Lovick said dangerously: "I knew you'd go too far one of these days and this is it. Outside, please."

"But I must point out—"

"Outside."

She promptly sat down, her back stiff with defiance. "I'll keep quiet, but I'm staying here. You may need me."

For a moment it was touch and go whether he ran her out by force or blew her out by exploding blood-pressure. Instead, he rounded on his unfortunate subordinate. "You've seen what's inside that hole?"

"No, sir. Only Mr. Breck—"

"I'll tell you what's inside," said Breck thinly. "A switch for turning off the heating upstairs and a can of

110

stink to squirt up through the floorboards. And if you want to know who shoved 'em there—"

" I heard you mention Dillinger."

" Then maybe you heard how I can prove it. Screwdriver on one o' the beams wi' his initials scratched. Take a look yourself an' see if I'm not right."

" Saunders, stay here by the door."

He stooped first to check the marks made by the steps. A minute later the treads creaked under his weight and Miss Purdy had to control a kindly instinct to rush forward and hold them steady in case it was construed as meddling. The lamp was still alight on the top step where Breck had left it. Picking it up, Lovick thrust it into the opening and there was a full minute's silence while he studied the interior. Withdrawing his head, he looked down at the builder.

" Touch anything?"

" Only the switch. Didn't know it was there. Felt it before I had the light."

" Screwdriver?"

" No, nor yet the other stuff neither."

Setting the lamp down on the nearest joist, Lovick reached out a long arm and took hold of the tool by the metal tip. Still standing on the steps, he turned it over to examine both sides of the handle before returning the challenging stare below. " Initials, you say?"

" That's right, an' don't be tellin' me they aren't there. I saw 'em. Leastways, I saw scratchings."

" They're here all right."

" There you are, then! What more do you want? Him an' that old witch—"

" Not so fast. They're the wrong initials."

" What!"

" Not ' H.D.' for Harvey Dillinger," said Lovick deliberately, " but ' W.B.'—for William Breck. So before you

111

start slinging accusations around you'd better start remembering where you leave your own tools."

Breck's jaw sagged. Carefully negotiating the steps while still holding the screwdriver by the tip, Lovick reached floor-level and held it out for his inspection, handle first.

" Don't touch. Just look. . . . Well?"

" It's mine all right," said the builder hollowly, "but I haven't lost—wait a minute!" He sucked breath. " Yes, I have, though, but not since—my stars!" He looked at Lovick, his dark eyes gleaming redly. " You know what? That's the one I lost just before Dillinger an' me cried quits. He swore he hadn't touched it an' it wasn't worth cryin' over so I let it go, but this *proves*—"

" You're saying this particular screwdriver has been in Dillinger's possession recently?"

" Aye, ever since we split up."

" And you haven't touched it during the interval?"

" Never set eyes on it again till—"

" Then I hope for your sake his prints are still on it. Though I don't think they will be. If he left it here to implicate you he'll have wiped it clean."

Breck looked at him for another moment, then spun round without warning, butted P.C. Saunders in the stomach and sent him crashing, eluded a boot thrust out to trip him and charged headlong down the stairs. The slam of the front door made their heads ring.

*　　*　　*

While Saunders set off in pursuit and Lovick began scattering orders into the phone, Miss Purdy judged it wise to make her own escape. A crisis of somebody else's nerves was the last thing she wanted, but in common charity she owed Miss Turnberry a visit and this seemed a diplomatic time to make it.

Before leaving she paused in front of the three dolls on her bedroom mantel-shelf. The ' Shirley ' doll was still sitting impassively behind the paperweight, and she stared back at it thoughtfully. With the upstairs phenomena reduced to physical terms, what about her own little mystery? Could Mrs. Sibley have engineered the doll-trick too? Not without actually entering the room, Miss Purdy decided, and she couldn't have done that unless—

Unless she'd had a key. An unpleasant idea which made Miss Purdy's blood run cold. And yet it could have happened quite easily. For use in emergency she kept a spare key on the outside ledge above the hall door, discreetly hidden but readily available to groping fingers. A stupid practice as Lovick had often told her, but it was so long since it had been used that she'd almost forgotten its existence. Hurrying out to the hall she reached up for it now. It was still there but—she was almost certain—a good six inches further to the left than it should have been. She had to sit down to conquer her anger and sense of outrage. The notion of such a woman having the run of her flat in her absence—

And there was more to it than that. Once inside, there'd have been a bonus in the shape of an unlocked desk drawer containing the master keys. No wonder Mrs. Sibley had been able to show her step-son and his ' wife ' round the top floor flat unsuspected. A simple question of timing. With new keys made from impressions, the whole house would have been as open to her as a fishmonger's slab.

Gradually her anger faded. After all, the real loser had been Mrs. Sibley herself. The how and the why of the doll-trick no longer mattered. Whatever you called the dark significance she'd attached to it—prophecy, threat or hoodoo—it had recoiled upon herself. The witch it was that died. . . .

Turning into the High Street a few minutes later, Miss

Purdy's feet dragged a little. All very well to dismiss the doll-incident as unimportant but Miss Turnberry had made the doll and she'd been a close friend of the dead woman's. How close? With Miss Turnberry's powers of exaggeration you never knew. Even Margery, her niece, had found something unhealthy and unbalanced in the association, and Miss Purdy was finding it increasingly hard to believe in a deep and genuine friendship. Lovick had said she'd gone into hysterics on hearing of the other's death, but she lived on the edge of hysteria anyway; she'd probably have done the same if a saucepan of milk had boiled over. Or was that doing her an injustice? Tired, confused and unhappy, Miss Purdy knew that conventional expressions of condolence would stick in her throat. She'd have given almost anything if she could have popped into the supermarket for fish fingers and a packet of detergent and gone straight back home.

But she wasn't a coward and the butcher's shop was just across the way. Nerving herself, she crossed the street and entered it. She'd never been inside Miss Turnberry's flat before and had to be directed to a side door which gave on to a flight of dark and narrow stairs. Mounting them slowly, she reflected that a flat over a butcher's shop was hardly an ideal residence for an elderly vegetarian of delicate and artistic sensibilities, as Miss Turnberry herself had often pointed out to anyone who bothered to listen. Because *really*, the smell of *blood*—and the proximity of all those poor dead *carcases*—but what with the housing situation— and of course one needn't *look* as one hurried in and out— and it was such a *relief* to reach the top of the stairs and shut the door on it all—the twittering phrases echoed in Miss Purdy's head as vividly as if she were actually hearing them.

She felt no relief herself on reaching the top of the stairs. All seemed quiet inside, which might merely mean that hysterics had given way to prostration. Bracing herself, she knocked and waited. After several seconds—during which she almost dared to hope that Miss Turnberry was fast asleep—she heard the latter's voice calling out with unexpected strength : " Who is it ?"

" Miss Purdy."

The door opened and warm gush flowed out. " Oh, my dear Miss Purdy ! *Do* come in ! How very kind—you see I'm all alone and doing my *darling* dolls. I don't know how I'd exist without—can you find a seat ? I'm *so* untidy except when—oh no, not there, let me move these papers from—that's better. Are you quite sure you're comfortable ?"

Her head in a whirl, Miss Purdy sat down on the hastily-cleared chintz-covered chair. This twittering, agitated, overdone welcome was the last sort of reception she'd expected. She might have been calling to deliver the Church magazine instead of making a visit of sympathy to the suddenly-bereaved. Miss Turnberry was a little red-eyed, it was true, but otherwise she seemed to be her usual silly prattling self, only more so. There was something off-key, exaggerated, unreal about her, almost as though she was caricaturing herself in a stage play. A natural result of shock ? Miss Purdy was more inclined to think she'd been tipped one step further towards lunacy. If I didn't know about last night's hysterics, she thought with genuine concern, I'd doubt if she'd even heard of Mrs. Sibley's death, let alone taken it in. . . .

' Untidy ' was a mild word to describe the room. Although large enough to house a great deal of old-fashioned furniture, it had difficulty in assimilating the appalling clutter. Every available surface was snowed under with scraps of material, reels of cotton, skeins of silk, jars of brushes, bottles of paint and tubes of gum, leaving very little space for actual living. A glance at the small working-table in front of the fire told Miss Purdy she'd interrupted

115

the delicate painting of a doll's face, a job requiring—one would have thought—steady hands and intense concentration, neither of which she'd expected to find here this morning. Bewildered and obscurely worried, she simply couldn't think of what to say.

Miss Turnberry, on the other hand, prattled away gaily. "*Dear* Miss Purdy, don't tell me, I can see you don't approve of my clutter. Your own flat—so *beautifully* neat—but I don't intend to stay here, you know." Folding her gawky figure into the chair at the work-table, she took up the doll and selected a needle-pointed brush with great care. "You don't mind if I carry on? The eyes, you know—a most difficult stage—"

"You're thinking of moving?"

"Oh yes, I've *quite* decided—that dreadful shop downstairs—and Margery—my niece, you know—such a delightful cottage, don't you think? And the poor child—so dreadfully *lonely*—it will be company for her."

"You're moving to *Witchwater*?"

"Of course, where else?"

"Does Margery know?" asked Miss Purdy faintly.

"Not yet, but I shall go over and tell her as soon as possible."

Her head was bent low over her work, revealing an intimate close-up of pink scalp under thinning grey hair, but there was nothing senile about the way the bony fingers gripped the brush. Suddenly Miss Purdy's nerve snapped. This bland ignoring of what had happened was undermining her own sense of balance.

"Miss Turnberry! There was a policewoman here last night."

"Oh yes, such a sweet girl, most *kind*—Phyllis, she said her name was."

"Then you know about Mrs. Sibley?"

And that was when she received the worst jolt yet. Miss

Turnberry's eyes fluttered upwards for a moment and something in their pink-rimmed depths—a glinting flicker of malice, almost of secret glee—

But she must have been mistaken. The head was bent low again, the quavering voice held nothing but distress. "*Need* you have reminded me? *Dear* Miss Purdy, that wasn't very kind. I've been crying all night, I simply can't *take* any more, I'm trying to forget it. My best friend— and all the fretting and fussing about her not being at the lecture yesterday—when *actually* she was lying out there on those dreadful marshes—"

" I'm sorry," said Miss Purdy helplessly.

Feeling desperately uncomfortable, she concentrated on the doll. It seemed to her—but this could have been imagination too—that the painted face was being coarsened by every stroke of the needle-fine brush. Of course the material must be incredibly difficult to work on, pale pink sateen stretched tight over stuffing, the whole figure no more than six inches long; but allowing for inescapable flatness Miss Turnberry usually succeeded in achieving a remarkable delicacy and sweetness of expression. This didn't seem to be the case now. The hair had already been sewn in position, lengths of fine silk twist unravelled but not yet shaped, in this instance a rather lovely shade of silver-grey. An odd choice, Miss Purdy thought fleetingly, but perhaps this was to be a ' granny ' doll. It was still unclothed but a nearby box contained patchwork pieces of all colours begged from dressmaking friends. Some of them were recognisable. The vicar's wife, for instance, had worn a dress of that daisy-patterned cotton last summer, and the poppy-strewn chiffon looked vaguely familiar too. There were even left-overs of grey silk which she herself had contributed after making a blouse. The sight of them gave her mind a peculiar jolt. She had an odd brief feeling that she herself was lying there. . . .

117

"Poor *darling* Sibyl." Miss Turnberry was being brave now in the face of sorrow. "You mustn't think I'm not *grieving*, but there comes a time when—I mean, one is so utterly *lost* and then—how can I explain it? Suddenly one realises how *selfish*—and I had just such a moment this morning, while I was drinking my herb-tea. Such a good thing for starting the day on, did I ever give you the recipe? One of my dear father's stand-bys, it made *all* the difference to his kidneys and—oh dear, where was I?"

"Drinking it," said Miss Purdy inadequately.

Miss Turnberry held up the doll at arm's length and narrowed her eyes at it critically. "A little more *colour*, do you think? In the cheeks, I mean." Her pale, thin-lashed eyes turned consideringly towards Miss Purdy as though comparing the two. "Yes, yes, a *little* more colour. . . ." Taking up another paint brush, she bent her head again and became absorbed in gaining the effect she wanted. "Herb-tea, of course. *Dear* Sibyl, it was almost as if she was standing in the kitchen with me—such a wonderfully *warm* feeling—as if she were telling me in so many words not to cry any more but to be *glad* for her. Ah, that's better." She eyed the doll fondly. "And now I must think of her clothes. *Not* the kind of weather to lie about naked, is it?"

Tittering slightly, she put the doll down too far away for Miss Purdy to see the face clearly. Not that she wanted to; she was beginning to feel a little sick. More than ever she was convinced that Mrs. Sibley's death had affected Miss Turnberry's brain. She'd rather have coped with screaming hysterics than this false, superficially-bright mood of business-as-usual.

The bony fingers were now rooting busily about among the patchwork pieces to find something suitable for the doll's dress, but Miss Purdy had the fatalistic feeling that she knew exactly what would be chosen and moreover, that

118

Miss Turnberry knew it too and the pretence of making a selection was pure play-acting. I can't let her go on with it, she thought desperately, yet how—

Was that a rattle at the letter-box?

Miss Turnberry looked up alertly. " The postman! But what a *peculiar* time—"

" Please—don't disturb yourself. I'll go." Jumping at the chance of a breather, Miss Purdy hurried out into the tiny hall and stopped for a moment to press her hand to her forehead, not at all sure her own sanity wasn't in question. If she'd been right just now—

And then she saw what lay on the mat. Not a letter or circular but another of Miss Turnberry's dolls, which must have been put through by hand. A black-haired doll dressed in poppy-strewn chiffon which she now remembered matched the blouse Suzi Barlow had worn with a chic red trouser-suit at the lecture yesterday. But the full truth didn't dawn on her until she picked it up. The cheeks were scored with slashes of red ink and an ordinary pin had been driven through the heart. . . .

Her next actions were purely automatic. The doll went into her pocket. She opened the door, but whoever had brought the doll had gone; the narrow staircase was empty, the door at the bottom shut. She returned to the room where Miss Turnberry was waiting expectantly.

" A letter?"

" No, nothing," Miss Purdy lied. " I looked out to make sure. It wasn't the postman. Perhaps the wind—"

" Or Sibyl," suggested Miss Turnberry brightly.

" *Mrs. Sibley?*"

" Indeed yes, she used to rattle the letter-box in *just* that way when she came calling. Wait!" She had returned to her box of patchwork pieces. Now she lifted her face, eyes closed raptly, lips partly open as though to sense an invisible presence. " Do you *feel*—"

119

"No!" said Miss Purdy explosively.

"Oh well, perhaps not." In a disconcerting return to matter-of-factness she bent over her box again. "Ah, this will do *splendidly*." She picked out a snippet of silk. "Such a pretty shade of grey, don't you think? Just like your own—but of course, how stupid of me! So very *kind*—it was you who *gave* it to me—"

"Miss Turnberry!"

"Yes?" Again that sly upward flicker, quickly veiled but now unmistakably malicious. It was all Miss Purdy could do to keep herself from snatching away the snippet by force. She swayed, simulating faintness.

"I'm sorry—I don't feel well. If I could have a glass of water—or perhaps some of that herbal mixture—"

"But of *course*!" Dropping the scrap of material back in the box, she hurried out to the kitchen. "The very *thing* for—not a moment to mix—and *so* beneficial—"

Tap-water ran and glass tinkled. Feverishly, Miss Purdy pounced on the grey-haired doll and stuffed it into her handbag together with every piece of her own grey silk she could lay hands on. Miss Turnberry was already returning with a tray. Miss Purdy didn't wait to make apologies. She bolted out of the room and down the stairs to the street as though the Devil himself was after her.

CHAPTER NINE

In the old days of Dillinger and Breck, Builders and Decorators, the firm had occupied the ground floor of a shabby shop just off the High Street, with living quarters for Dillinger and his wife above and a cramped work-shed taking up most of the space at the back, but with Harvey Dillinger in sole possession things had changed. His rapidly-growing affluence and status were reflected in shining new paint, large plate-glass windows, modern office fitments, a bottle-blonde typist who liked to call herself a receptionist, and extensive new work-buildings a hundred yards up the road. He still lived above the 'shop' but the late Mrs. Dillinger (whose mother had kept a fish-and-chip emporium) wouldn't have recognised the flat in its present tarted-up condition. Nor would Breck if he'd ever been given the chance to make comparisons. But since the split nearly two years earlier, his contact with the old place had been limited to passing by on the opposite pavement muttering uncomplimentary epithets under his breath.

This morning, however, the white door with gilt lettering swung open to his violent push and he erupted into the office like an avenging angel, causing the receptionist's nail-file to slip and scrape flesh. Her unladylike squeal shattered months of carefully-built-up sophistication.

" Ow! What d'y'think you're doing? Just look at my—"

" Where's Dillinger?"

" Out." She sucked the scraped finger, imbibing more silver nail-polish than blood. " And a good thing too if you

121

come bursting into people's offices like—"

"Stuff it, girl, I'm not playing games, I want the bastard quick. Where is he?"

"I'm sure I don't know."

"And I'm bloody sure you do. So unless you want the police here—"

"The police?"

"You heard."

She looked frightened now. "But what—why—"

"Never you mind, just tell me where I can find him."

"I think he said something about going to Mr. Wetherby's. At least, they were talking on the phone and—"

"Wetherby—the book-shop?"

"Yes, but I'm sure they wouldn't want—"

But he'd already gone. Not by the street door but through the back of the house where the service lane provided a short cut to the High Street.

Thoroughly alarmed, she allowed her hand to hover over the phone. Should she or should she not ring the book-shop and warn them of a madman on the way? If only she had some idea what it was all about—

Either way spelt trouble. She couldn't warn the boss without disclosing that she'd leaked his whereabouts, and if she didn't warn him he'd hit the roof later on and probably sack her on the spot. And with that talk of police—

At which point the police arrived in a highly perturbed state and pulled up in front of her, breathing hard.

"Where's Breck?"

"Gone, and if you want to know what I think—"

She stopped because P.C. Saunders wasn't listening. At least, not to her. His ears were cocked for sounds of argument or mayhem elsewhere; if Breck wasn't after his ex-partner's guts he didn't know murder when he saw it. Everything seemed quiet but that meant damn-all, and when his eye fell on the highly-polished cantilevered staircase which had been incorporated in the new decor he took a purposeful step towards it. "Upstairs?"

"No!" With an unexpected skip she barred his way. "You can't go up there! It's private. The boss would kill me if—"

"Is Mr. Dillinger up there?"

"No, there's nobody here but me. Mr. Breck was here for a minute but he said he had to see him and—"

"Where?"

"Oh dear! I don't know if I ought—"

"I'd hate to run you in for obstruction," said Saunders meaningfully, and she gave in, bursting into tears.

"W-Wetherby's b-book-shop. How w-was I to know—"

"Thanks."

He didn't know the short cut, and rather than muck about looking for one he shot back into the street and took the long way round, thereby missing not only Dillinger and Breck but the wizened Mr. Wetherby as well.

*　　*　　*

Lovick got back to the office to find Superintendent Vallance breathing fire over one of the more lurid national dailies.

"Oh, there you are, Lovick. What's all this damned crap about witchcraft?"

"Crap's the right word, sir. Pack of fools playing at black magic."

"But this broomstick business—"

"Window-dressing. She was no more a witch than my left foot. There's no magic about plastic squeezers and illicit switches." Concisely, he described the discoveries in the ceiling cavity of Mrs. Sibley's flat. "Those tiles, sir, were put up by Dillinger, the builder, to her order. Which doesn't make him a wizard or a warlock but does make

123

him a party to her plan to get the youngsters out."

"Fingerprints?"

"Only hers, but the screwdriver is a giveaway. Breck swears he hasn't seen it since the partnership was dissolved. If that's true it was left there to incriminate him, making it look as though he did the job while installing the top-floor heating."

"Which he could have done," the Super pointed out. "To cast suspicion on Dillinger in case of trouble. If there's bad blood between them it works both ways."

"True, sir, but Dillinger's had all the good luck and Breck all the bad. If either's in league with a so-called witch I'll plump for the one getting something out of it. Which reminds me—" Frowning, he looked at his watch. "Breck's taken it badly and he's out for blood. Saunders should be back with him by now. We don't want another killing on our hands."

"You're satisfied the Sibley death was murder?"

"Until I learn different. Conscious or unconscious, she was alive when she hit the ground. She could have jumped, I suppose, but—"

"High on LSD, perhaps," suggested the Super, "and imagined—"

"Not according to the preliminary lab. report." Fishing out one of the papers on his desk, Lovick handed it to him. "No signs of dope, and that bit about extra bruising is significant. They won't commit 'emselves yet but it's likely she had a crack on the head at least half-an-hour before death. In which case—"

"Somebody took her up unconscious and dropped her."

"Exactly, with the dyke-drawer's broom for good measure. Either way a plane's involved and I'll lay odds it was Major Barlow's helicopter." He explained about the discrepancies in the various stories. "All that's still got to be sorted out and I'll have another go at the pilot, but if it wasn't somewhere where it shouldn't have been, why any discrepancy at all?"

"You're not saying the major's involved?"

"Not unless he's a damned good actor. My sergeant's out there now, getting his version."

"What about marks of its landing?"

"It's put down and taken off at least twice since then, thanks to the local sergeant not wanting to get his feet wet," said Lovick with justifiable bitterness. "And if the pilot wanted to cover up a landing the night before, he'd take damned good care to hit the same spot as near as possible. Ground's still being examined but I doubt if we'll prove anything that way."

"This second death—Barlow's grand-daughter—on the wild side, from all I've heard of her."

"Drugs, anyhow, and no morals to speak of. And I'll lay odds she was one of the mob at St. Edred's—explains why the chopper was taken out. But I'm keeping an open mind about her death. Chances are it was pure accident. Running away from a blessed cat."

"*Cat*?"

"She was pathologically afraid of 'em, and this one savaged her."

"He'll have to be destroyed."

"He will be, sir. And the Press will make a meal of it."

"Tough luck on the major," said Vallance heavily. "Suppose I'd better go and have a word with him. Met him at the Lord Mayor's dinner a while back. Nice chap, bit of a bore but well-meaning. Couple of calls to make first. I'll take him in on the way back."

He'd barely left when Sergeant Stebbings arrived after his own interview with the major. There was still no absolute proof that the helicopter had been out of its hangar on Tuesday night. "Major swears it couldn't have been taken up without his knowledge, sir. Sleeps light as a cat, he says, and he'd have heard it if——"

" I've known cats you couldn't wake with a ton of dynamite. And that pompous old twitterer——"

" Of course, sir, he could have been lying, if he was one of the party himself. Though somehow I can't imagine——"

" Shut up a minute and let me think."

Stebbings waited patiently. Good view of Wrexley Broad through the side window. Funny to think those white sails in the sunshine and that duck and her brood belonged to the same world as blood-dripping cocks and maniacal devil-cats. . . .

Lovick wasn't concerned with white sails or ducks, he was wondering about Major Barlow. Either the bloke went out like a light the moment his head hit the pillow, or he was a flaming liar and knew perfectly well the chopper had been taken up. The hangar stood within fifty yards of the house and nobody in his right mind could have missed hearing it under ordinary circumstances. There was of course a third alternative (if you could have alternatives in threes) and that was that the chopper really hadn't been out of the hangar and the Newmarket tale was simply a cover-up for a smooching-session between Suzi and young Daw, but if you allowed that you had to allow that Mrs. Sibley had attained a height of two or three hundred feet under broomstick-power, which might have qualified her for some sort of man-powered prize but which Lovick dismissed sweepingly as tripe. Surely *somebody* must have heard——

" What about the servants?"

" Only ones living in, sir, are a married couple in their seventies who're both——"

" Don't tell me. Stone-deaf. They would be. What about the villagers, then?"

But there was no help there either. Lindham, where Donzell's police cottage was situated and where the black cock came from, was a good half-mile off, not exactly out of earshot but far enough away to rob the noise of any particular interest or curiosity value. Folks were used to aircraft going over, they went to bed early, and ten to one if anyone had heard the chopper they'd taken it as just one more dratted noise in the night and turned over and gone to sleep again, forgetting all about it by now.

" What about Donzell himself? If he's so blasted efficient, why didn't he hear anything?"

" Says he was gardening all the evening, sir, and turned in early for once."

" Pity he doesn't pay less attention to his hollyhocks and more to his duties." Lovick picked up the newspaper the Super had discarded and scowled at the offending head-line. " 'DEATH ON A BROOMSTICK '—of all the flaming tripe. Damned broomstick had nothing to do with it except to add colour and confuse the issue. If I could prove that chopper was there—"

" Does it have to be the Barlow chopper, sir?"

Lovick glared at him. " You suggesting she was flown in from Timbuctoo starkers except for a black cloak?"

" No, sir, but Norwich is only—"

" She didn't live in Norwich, she lived here in Wrexley. So did the cock, as near as makes no odds, and St. Edred's is in my manor. So is Witchwater. And that flaming cat. The whole thing stinks of Wrexley."

" Yes, sir, but—"

" Look," said Lovick dangerously, " I don't care who heard it or didn't hear it, I'll swear it was Barlow's chopper she was dropped from. Who was flying it is another matter. Wouldn't put it past the major himself, weak heart or no weak heart, except that he's too much of a fool to keep his mouth buttoned up afterwards. My money's on young Daw with Suzi's connivance, or more likely on her instruc-tions. They certainly didn't go to Newmarket, and if I can prove they did go to St. Edred's—"

"You think he was mixed up in the voodoo carry-on?"

"He's a Daw, isn't he? And the Daws have been fancy-ing 'emselves in that line from the year dot. I'll admit he doesn't look the type but he knows a sight more about Tuesday night than he's let on so far, and it's high time we had another talk."

He pressed the buzzer for P.C. Cocker.

*　　*　　*

Cocker was looking slightly haggard. He hadn't enjoyed the few solitary hours he'd spent at Witchwater last night awaiting the Daws' return home. Neither had Elimauzer who, returning first, had strongly objected to being shut in the cupboard by a strange policeman. Half a bottle of Dettol applied in the privacy of his own bathroom hadn't quite removed Cocker's dread of supernatural contamina-tion from a series of vicious scratches, but he was trying not to let it show. He was taken aback, therefore, when Lovick, eyeing him narrowly, demanded abruptly what he was looking so sour about.

"Sir?"

"Cat get home last night?"

"Yes, sir. One-fifteen a.m."

"Have any trouble with it?"

"Nothing to speak of, sir," lied Cocker heroically.

"Good. Then if you've got over your war-wounds you can go straight back there and fetch young Daw. I want him here pronto."

Alone again, Lovick picked up the paper whose lurid headlines had annoyed the superintendent and skimmed through a fairly accurate but highly-coloured account of the vandalism at the ruined abbey, including a romanti-cised interview with the old marshman who'd discovered

128

it and (Lovick swore at this) a re-hash of the Witchwater murder several years ago. What they'd say when they got round to the Barlow girl—

Trust Donzell to get a mention. Way this guff read, you'd think it was he who'd worn his feet out tramping over those blessed marshes, and that he'd tied the cock-feathers to Mrs. Pegg's lost rooster by means of brilliant deduction instead of having the thing dropped in his lap as a gift. Serve him right if the Super's imminent visit to Lindham caught him with his pants down. For a moment, indeed, Lovick was tempted to let him take his chance, but loyalty won. He picked up the phone.

" Done any good gardening lately?" he asked nastily.

" Gardening?" Donzell sounded genuinely mystified. " Not since Tuesday—oh."

" Exactly. First time anything serious happens I'm told you're too worn out to notice."

" Sir, I—"

" Never mind excuses. Just don't let the Super catch you asleep, that's all. On his way now—visit of condolence to the major. Found out yet who pinched that cock?"

" That, sir, is precisely what I was just typing a report about." An incautious note of smugness crept into his voice. " If you want a short answer—"

" Try giving me a long one and see what happens."

" Very well, sir, the short answer is Miss Barlow."

" *What* !"

" Miss Barlow stole Mrs. Pegg's cock, sir. I took a look at the chicken run yesterday and found several good foot-prints in the—er—mud."

" If you mean chicken-manure, say so."

" Yes, sir. Mrs. Pegg's were clear enough, flat-heeled slippers, I checked those straight away. Which left imprints of a woman's high-heeled shoes and others indicating a male accomplice. Mrs. Pegg is a widow, sir, and lives

129

alone, so—"

" All right, you don't have to spell it out. You've checked with the Barlow girl's shoes?"

" Of course, sir. Also with the major's, but his are size eight and the intruder's are definitely nines. I haven't had time to check further but I'm of the opinion—"

" When did you do this checking?"

" Yesterday evening, sir, about a quarter-past six. The matter being up in the air then, as you might say, I thought it best not to approach the major or Miss Barlow personally but to have a word with Ethel first."

" Ethel?"

" Their maid, sir. By way of being a friend of mine. Luckily the shoes Miss Barlow had worn the night before were still downstairs waiting to be cleaned. Not only did they correspond with the casts I'd made, sir, but there were plain traces of mud—chicken manure—between soles and uppers and round the heels. I didn't need to see the major's. As soon as Ethel mentioned the size—"

" What put you on to Suzi in the first place?"

And a fine mixture of prejudice and nosiness that turned out to be, Lovick thought disgustedly as he hung up a few minutes later. Efficiency his foot! Bloke had clicked a winner by sheer accident. He'd gone straight for Suzi because he'd disapproved of her from the start, what with her sinful record and her unconcealed dislike of his sycophantic visits to Bilby Hall. Naturally he hadn't put it like that, he'd merely remarked austerely that nobody else in Lindham or near it would have been silly enough to wear high heels while stealing chickens, which was probably true but couldn't be called detection.

Anyhow, it served Lovick's purpose, setting her bang at St. Edred's on Tuesday night; at least putting her in cahoots with that scaly mob. She hadn't stolen a black cock for fun. And if Kenneth Daw's footprints didn't match up with those others he'd eat his helmet. No wonder she'd been in a hurry to see him privately last night. Let alone the need to square up the discrepancies in their stories, no Ethel in the world could be counted on to keep quiet about those shoes. It had been imperative to concoct a tale to cover their presence in Mother Pegg's chicken run without involving themselves either in black magic or Mrs. Sibley's death. And if they could have done that, thought Lovick grimly, they'd almost deserved to get away with it.

Another thing, those high heels accounted for the use of the helicopter. Even a town-bred tart like Suzi Barlow wouldn't have been mug enough to wear 'em for a long trek over the marshes, with or without a pal to help carry the live cock. Especially if she and her escort had been dressed (or undressed) like Mrs. Sibley. The helicopter was the obvious answer—door-to-door transport, pilot handy, embarkation and take-off completely private.

Major Barlow?

Lovick considered him again.

No, he still couldn't see him in on the deal. Take more finesse than the old codger was capable of to carry off the discovery next morning with such airy-fairy innocence. Besides, he'd hardly have presented the police with Mrs. Pegg if he'd known his own grand-daughter was involved.

Come to think of it, hadn't he mentioned being awakened from a sound sleep to transport Donzell to the scene? That seemed to settle it. Couple of sleeping-tablets in his bedtime cocoa and he needn't have known anything about it. Probably been out like a light the whole blessed night.

Satisfied with his reading of the Barlow angle, he turned his attention to the rest of the mob. They'd probably made up a coven or whatever, which meant—how many? A baker's dozen? He ran over a list of possible candidates in his mind.

131

Sibley, Suzi and young Daw, for sure. And very likely the gang behind the rebuilding of Witchwater and the installation of Daws there, complete with silver-collared cat. Which brought in Dillinger and Begbie, to say nothing of that blessed Antiquarian Society Miss Purdy had stumbled on. You couldn't want a better cover than that for hanky-panky in secluded ruins, especially if you could rope in a few blameless parties like the vicar and his wife for camouflage.

Where the devil had Stebbings put that list of members he'd been told to get? Ah, here it was, under the coffee cup. Same old names—Sibley, both Barlows, Dillinger, Begbie, Turnberry—

Miss Turnberry.

A nutter if ever there was one, the only person in Wrexley (far as he knew) likely to shed tears over Mrs. Sibley. Who *had* shed tears last night, according to the W.P.C. who'd spent most of the night there; hysterical tears mixed with eldritch laughter which had yielded only to a doctor armed with a couple of strong sleeping pills. She'd flatly refused to believe in the broomstick bit, insisting it was all a wicked plot to discredit her poor dear friend who'd never harmed a fly.

Well, you could take that how you liked. She was simple enough on the surface to believe almost anything, though you'd think it 'ud take a positive moron to become intimate with a woman and not discover the most fundamental thing about her. On the other hand, Miss Turnberry had a very ancient and fishlike smell herself and only needed a pointed hat and black cloak to be the spitting image of the witch in ' Hansel and Grethel ' as portrayed in his long-ago childhood, the one who used to burn kids in ovens if his memory hadn't let him down. Given him nightmares, that one had, and while he wasn't accusing Miss Turnberry of burning kids in ovens he was very definitely of the opinion that she'd bear looking into. He made a note to find out if she had an alibi for Tuesday night.

Next on the list? Oh yes, Wetherby, that fancy book-seller in the High Street, gnome-faced squitty little know-all who looked like somebody's grandfather until you remembered he'd once escaped conviction by the skin of his teeth for trading in hard porn as well as classy first editions. Come to think of it, he *was* somebody's grandfather, lad of fifteen expelled from an expensive private school in Cromer last year for pushing pot among his class-mates. Respectable his foot. All very well for Miss Purdy to say hands off the Antiquarians; she hadn't been down in that musty cellar where Wetherby kept the most 'curious' of his extensive collection, and Lovick had. Wonderful what a gloss a fancy name, the vicar and a few creams buns could put on a so-called learned society. More he thought about it, more he wanted a run-down on all its members with especial reference to where they spent their nights. He hadn't the slightest difficulty in picturing that old goat Wetherby, for instance, cavorting starkers with a gaggle of fat and skinny she-goats under the stars. . . .

Still, granted their united innocence, who else had an interest in Mrs. Sibley and her goings-on, especially in wanting her out of the way?

Not far to look for that. Step-son and his girl friend stuck out a mile, and after that letter of his Max Sibley would have a hard job pretending they didn't know what she was up to. Point was, did their knowledge include the capers at the abbey? Up to them to prove it didn't, thought Lovick grimly. By which token, why weren't they here proving it now? They'd been told of her death last night and young Sibley had promised to be here first thing for a formal identification of the body, and 'first thing' in Lovick's book didn't mean nearly lunch time. What in

133

heck was he up to? He didn't have to love his stepmother but he was next-of-kin and probably stood to inherit the lot, and if he hadn't had *some* feeling for her he'd hardly have agreed to live in the same house. So why the delay? You'd have thought curiosity would have made him put a spurt on, if nothing else. That is, if his conscience was clear.

But was it?

Nothing against the pair of 'em being part of Tuesday night's coven, as far as Lovick could see. Eight-mile drive from Norwich and a brisk hike over the marshes—nothing to it provided they didn't share his corns. And once there—with a helicopter parked nice and handy—

Lovick grew thoughtful.

Black magic, so-called, was a pretty good camouflage for a simple case of plain murder for gain. Everybody else's attention otherwise engaged, and nobody anxious for his or her identity to come to police ears afterwards. Why, they needn't even have known the young Sibleys were there; those long hooded cloaks and masks would have covered up the Devil himself, and the rest of 'em might be in a muck-sweat at this moment, wondering which of 'em had taken her up. Could explain why the broomstick had been dropped with her; to tie her up to the coven and turn suspicion away from outsiders. Assuming the young Sibleys *were* outsiders, taking advantage of the shenanigans without being part of 'em.

More he thought about it, more he liked the idea. That broomstick had worried him more than he'd cared to admit even to himself. Not that he'd thought for a minute anybody had been riding it, he'd simply wondered why any or all of the gang should have advertised their own misdoings by providing such a direct link with 'em. But once you brought in an outsider with an axe of his own to grind—

134

A knock at the door roused him. " Come in."

Talk of the Devil. Young Mr. Sibley had arrived to keep his appointment.

And I'll bet he's a weirdo, thought Lovick with conviction as the door opened.

He was right.

CHAPTER TEN

A weirdo, in Lovick's book, was anyone of either gender with too much hair, something dangling round the neck and a connection with the muck that passed these days for Art.

Both Lomax Sibley and his 'wife' qualified with knobs on, to use his own old-fashioned phrase. Sibley claimed to be some sort of writer and heaven alone knew what that covered, while Zenna Deane, judging from the grotesque but colourful floor-length oddments she was smothered in, was a dab hand at crochet and patchwork with a bit of leather-thonging thrown in. Young Sibley was dressed more reasonably but still scruffily in an ancient Aran pullover and jeans, but both wore sandals and the inevitable chain and pendant. Hair was plentifully divided between them with the balance in favour of the male. The one thing young Sibley wasn't was young; forty if a day, thought Lovick, putting him within fifteen years of his stepmother. The only intriguing thing about him was that behind the yellowish fly-away whiskers lurked a thin long face with pale grey wide apart eyes that struck a teasingly familiar chord in his memory, one that he was quite unable to pin down. Certainly there was no resemblance to Mrs. S.—but come to think of it there wouldn't be, since there was no blood-relationship.

The woman's face was plain nondescript, with an unkind emphasis on 'plain', though she had a good pair of brown eyes and mightn't have looked too bad with her hair cut short and fluffed out a bit instead of hanging down her back, a style for which (in Lovick's opinion) she was at least ten years too old. While civilly inviting them to sit down he reflected that Miss Purdy had been luckier than she knew. With this pair in the top flat as well as Mrs. Sibley—

But maybe he was wronging them. Maybe they were respectable, honest, intelligent citizens and a credit to everybody but their mirrors. And maybe cats are purple and pigs can fly. . . .

One thing, Sibley had already identified his stepmother's remains under Stebbings' unemotional eye, so they could now get down to business. Completely unhampered, he noticed, by any signs of grief on the part of the bereaved.

After some meaningless condolences, Lovick began briskly. "Am I right, sir, in thinking you're the son of the late Laurence Sibley of Northampton by a previous marriage?"

"No."

Lovick looked at him sharply, suspecting he was trying to be funny. Deciding he liked him even less than he'd thought at first, he asked forthrightly: "How come you're calling yourself Mrs. Sibley's stepson, then?"

"I'm not calling myself anything. You are. I don't know or care if it's a legal step-relationship. I'm Dad's son all right, at least he brought me up from scratch and acknowledged paternity, but he and my mother, whoever she is, forgot to go to church first. In other words, I'm a bastard."

Damn right you are, thought Lovick, all his previous mistrust hardening at the covert insolence in the man's slightly high-pitched drawl. Aloud he said: "You don't know your mother's identity?"

"No."

"But Sibyl did," said Zenna unexpectedly.

Lovick looked at her. "And you made no move to find out?"

"Oh yes, but she wouldn't let on. She was like that, she loved hugging secrets. Ask her and she'd spit in your face."

Lovick's pale blue gaze returned to Sibley. "Weren't you interested?"

"Not since I was a kid. Who needs mothers?"

"You do, apparently, or at least a stepmother, since you agreed to live in the same house."

"Who told you that?"

"We found one of your letters."

"Oh well, it was her idea, not mine. And anything's better than the hole in a slum where we are now."

"Why did she want you here?"

"Why not? If it's of any interest, the last time she came to see us in Norwich she described our pad with remarkable accuracy as a pig-sty. Hardly a do-gooder, our Sibyl, but a rescue operation's just possible, don't you think?"

"When was this?"

"Her visit? After Christmas but before—oh, ask Zenna, she's better at these things than I am. Usually counts back from her last lover-boy. Simple and effective. They average one a month."

"Don't be so silly, Max," said Zenna brusquely. "It was back in February, Inspector. She'd been shopping and dropped in for a meal. Told us she'd just got this flat and was pretty sure we could have the top one—anyway, she was working on it. And that's all, except that Max had a letter saying it 'ud take more time than she'd reckoned on as the landlady was one of these pious types, but give her another few days and we could start packing."

Lovick's eyes were hard. "Another couple were in by then. How did she intend to get them out?"

138

Max gave a high-pitched titter. "Mind over matter, Inspector. She had a will like a bulldozer. No opposition stood a chance."

"Are you suggesting—"

Zenna said harshly : "She was a witch."

Lovick's senses prickled. "You mean you believe in this broomstick business?"

"Of course not, that's baby-stuff. It went deeper than that. Thought-transference, odylic force, magnetism—I don't know. But it wasn't safe to cross her. Like that man near Peterborough who—"

"Shut up, Zenna!" ordered Max with sudden authority.

"Oh, be your age, she's dead now and can't hurt us. And anyway it was in the papers at the time, he's only got to look it up." Her eyes went back to Lovick. "This man cheated old Laurence Sibley over a deal, or it could have been the other way round, Max's father trying to pull a fast one; anyway it ended in the man going bankrupt and committing suicide, leaving a note swearing Sibyl had put the Evil Eye on him. And after that—"

"*Shut up*!" Max swung on her with an intensity only just short of actual violence. She cringed and her lips shut tight. So he can be effective, sometimes, thought Lovick, looking at him with renewed interest. And he's touchy about witchcraft though he doesn't mind sounding off about the old girl's will-power. . . . Peterborough? Might be worth looking up though he'd bet it was more a case of jiggery-pokery than evil eyes, like the jiggery-pokery—smells and such—by which possession of the top flat was to be secured, and which, incidentally, this pair knew all about according to Sibley's letter, though neither had thought fit to mention it.

Another omission occurred to Lovick and he proceeded to remedy it. "How did you like the top flat, Miss Deane?"

139

" Very—" She stopped abruptly. " How did you know we'd seen it ?"

" Mr. Sibley's letter."

" So she invited us over to see the place," drawled Max. " What's wrong with that ?"

" With the owner's permission ?"

" I didn't ask. She led, we followed. Showed us over the whole house."

" Miss Purdy's flat too ?" asked Lovick incredulously.

" That's right, everybody else was out and we had a free hand. Sibyl's always enjoyed poking round. The ground-floor bedroom was a giggle. This row of dolls on the mantelpiece—she dropped one in the hearth to give the old trout something to think about. Softening her up, you might say. Nice psychology and all good clean fun."

" How did you get in ?"

" She had keys."

" And how," asked Lovick carefully, " did she get hold of them ?"

Max shrugged. " Don't ask me. After all, we were going to live there. We had a right—"

" No right whatever without Miss Purdy's permission, and that goes for the top flat too. As far as the Law's concerned you were all three trespassing on enclosed premises. Did you touch anything ?"

" Like what ?"

" Like anything apart from this doll."

" Oh dear ! Should we have worn gloves ?"

Lovick's fists itched. This drawling insolence was very hard to take. " You know perfectly well what I mean, and I should perhaps warn you—"

" Oh, for Pete's sake get on with it. What do the other flats matter now ? It's the middle one we'll be taking over and you can't deny our right to enter that. As sorrowing relatives—"

" Are you Mrs. Sibley's heir?"

" Lock, stock and barrel. The old man's money was left in trust for me. All she got was the income for life. She couldn't have cut me off even if she'd wanted to."

Zenna said suddenly: " Like to bet?"

He glared at her. " Meaning what? It's all tied up legally."

" And there's a tame solicitor in her pocket. What's his name? Begbie. She used to boast he'd do anything she said. Suppose they'd put their heads together and found a way round it?"

" Codswallop."

" Is it? Maybe that's why she wanted you here—part of some scheme to do you out of it—"

" What scheme?"

" How should I know? But I never did believe in step-motherly love. And the more I think about it the more I'm sure there was some catch to it, especially if she was serious about getting married. She wouldn't have wanted you under her feet after—"

" Hold it!" commanded Lovick, breaking into the argument without ceremony. These two were obviously used to wrangling without regard to company and couldn't do too much of it from his point of view, but this was too important to pass without comment. " Are you saying Mrs. Sibley was thinking of marrying again?" He sounded incredulous and felt it. That fat, evil old harridan—

But Zenna insisted it was true. " I don't know his name, but she kept hinting—"

" Balls!" interrupted Max rudely.

" You heard her yourself—"

" Just a crazy fancy she got. It wouldn't have come to anything. It didn't mean—"

She blazed out at him. " That's typical, you never believe anything you don't want to. Why don't you take your blinkers off? She was a foul cantankerous old devil but she was human, wasn't she? And had as much right to fall in love as you have."

"If you call it love."

"I don't care what you call it, she'd got her hooks into him and meant to have him. Nothing you could say or do would have stopped her. If you ask me we've had a lucky escape. In the same house—under her thumb—" Her plain face was white now with a new-born panic. "My stars! What couldn't she have done!"

"It was you that wanted the bloody flat. Cracking on about the view and—"

"Only at first, I got carried away, who wouldn't? But underneath—Max, it didn't last, I was frightened sick, she made my skin crawl, it was like selling our souls for—for—" Breath choked her. "Don't you see? Whatever she was planning we wouldn't have stood a chance. She could have murdered us as easily as she'd turned those smells on and then she'd have scooped the lot, capital and all, never mind Begbie. And—and we nearly walked right into it."

"I still say you're bonkers." But he was shaken and showed it.

Lovick pressed his advantage. "You must have some idea who—"

"Well, I haven't. Like Zenna says, it was just hints and innuendoes. Nothing tangible. I thought she was joking."

"But if she wasn't?"

"Then it was one of those damned Antiquarians she was running around with. Begbie or Dillinger or—"

"Not Begbie," interrupted Zenna tightly. "He's already married."

"You think that would have stopped her?"

"Maybe not, but—" She halted suddenly. "I'll tell you one thing, Inspector, there was a girl involved, somebody

142

who'd have to be dealt with first. Dealt with. Those were her words. And then she chuckled and patted my knee and told me not to worry, it was just a manner of speaking. I was scared silly."

" When you say ' girl '—"

" Girl—woman—I'm not sure, it could have been anyone. Begbie's wife, even. No use pestering me. I just don't know."

Which left the field wide open, of course. Lovick's knuckle drummed on the desk. Only one ' girl ' among the Antiquarians that he knew of and she'd been 'dealt with ' good and proper. Was it remotely possible that this so-called witch had reached out from the dead and, working through the cat, had—

Baloney. Even a dead witch couldn't have set Suzi Barlow on the marshes within reach of those claws against her will. The thing was coincidence pure and simple. Nothing more.

Begbie's wife? He'd met her once at some do or other—dried-up nervous little woman with a face like a wrinkled prune. He couldn't imagine much opposition from that quarter; one bite and the Sibley woman would have swallowed her whole.

But there are more ways than one of being an impediment. Nuisance value, for instance, and on those grounds you couldn't rule out even Miss Turnberry, a potential land-mine to friend or enemy if ever there was one.

More important was the identity of the prospective bridegroom. Begbie was merely a guess. Anyone among those blessed Antiquarians—or more precisely the particular oddballs who'd formed the coven—

Who needn't have been Antiquarians at all, he realised suddenly. At least, not all of 'em. Mistake to take that for granted. These two, for example. . . .

He said, with deceptive smoothness : " Where were you

on Tuesday night, Mr. Sibley?"

"Tuesday night? At home, I suppose, or—" The penny dropped. The long thin face with its yellowish mane (and who does he remind me of, wondered Lovick again) grew ugly. "If you're talking about the night she died—"

"Routine, sir, for everyone connected with the case."

"Bloody liberty, if you ask me. All the same, I don't mind putting the record straight. Neither Zenna nor I set eyes on her after our visit here in March. We were not at that witches' Sabbat on the marshes and the only use we've got for broomsticks is to sweep our private messes under the carpet. Any more questions?"

"If you weren't at St. Edred's on Tuesday, where were you?"

"That's our affair."

"And mine. If you've got an alibi I want to hear it."

"Suppose I say we were both at home watching the box?"

"*Do* you say that?"

"No, we don't," broke in Zenna sharply. "You're a damned fool, Max, half a dozen people could call us liars and we'd end up in the dock. We were at home, Inspector, that's true enough, but holding a seance. A private seance. Max has this special gift—"

"What gift?"

Sibley's pale eyes glinted maliciously. "You'll have to look it up in the dictionary. Or shall I save you the trouble? It's called psychometry, which being translated means—"

"Thanks. I went to school too."

"Bully for you."

Lovick considered him for a few moments in silence. Psychometry his grandmother, odds were they'd worked up some sort of music hall stunt between 'em—folks handing over an article belonging to the dear departed and

144

Zenna letting information drop by code so that Max could go into his 'miraculous' guessing act. Still, if half a dozen mugs could vouch for the fact that they were being swindled in Norwich on Tuesday evening, the couple were in the clear for Mrs. Sibley's demise in spite of a whacking great inheritance motive. All the same—

"Let's give it a test. Shut your eyes and see what you can make of this." Pulling open a drawer of his desk, he drew out a small object carved in wood and pushed it into Sibley's hand.

It stayed there for perhaps half a second. Then, with a violent twist of the wrist, it was flung across the room and in the same movement Max was on his feet, his face contorted. "You damned swine! It's alive! Where's the bloody loo? I'm going to be—be—"

Lovick's chair scraped back. Taking his arm, he fairly ran him out of the room, shouting for a constable. Returning alone, he found Zenna standing by her chair, swaying a little, her face chalk-white, her horror-filled gaze riveted to the thing on the floor.

"What is it? That—that—"

Lovick picked it up and turned it over, displaying the carving that had hung over Mrs. Sibley's bed. It wasn't a true crucifix but an obscene carving of a grinning devil clinging with glee to a blasphemous mockery of a cross. As he held it out he could have sworn an electric shock ran up his arm. Imagination, of course—sheer flaming fantasy—power of suggestion or something—

But he wasn't sorry to drop it on the desk and send out for a good strong pot of tea.

*　　*　　*

When Max got back he still looked a little greenish, though he was in a more chastened mood and seemed glad of the tea. He would have avoided the subject of the carving if possible, just as his eyes avoided the thing itself, but Lovick kept him on the rails.

" You've seen it before?"

" In her bedroom."

" Where does it come from?"

" Haiti."

" Haiti?"

" If you must know it was the start of the whole damned business. This so-called witchcraft, I mean. She wasn't a witch. Power-mad and evil, if you like, but not a witch, though it wasn't for want of trying. It began before my father died. When I was ten—maybe eleven—anyway, just out of prep. school—he took us on a Caribbean cruise, stopping off in Haiti for a couple of days. Her idea of fun. I loathed it. For weeks beforehand she'd been filling me up with tales of Voodoo, and when it came to the point I was scared rigid. Dad had business contacts there and she took me to this place alone. A cave—dark—fires burning—blacks dancing and singing—" He took out a handkerchief and mopped his brow. " Sibyl revelled in it but the odd thing was that nothing really clicked for her, while for me—the top priest rubbed a couple of bones over my hand and muttered a few words and—it happened."

" What did?"

" Power. The sort she'd have given her eyes for. Psychometry. I suppose I'd always had it but this was the first time it surfaced. He gave me a sapphire ring to hold. Man, was I terrified! The cave went black and I was on the open beach. This girl—she was tied to a stake with fire beginning to lick her skirts. Flames ran up her thighs and I saw the flesh shrivel and brown like barbecued chops. The smell of burning hair—the sound of her screams—" His voice rose to a tortured scream. " Damn it, do you have to remind me? She was wearing the ring. All her

146

torment and agony and terror—they were mine too. I threw the ring at the priest and ran back to the hotel as if the devil was chasing me. And—I think he was. I've never known real peace since."

The affectation, the insolence, were gone. For the first time he came over as an ordinary vulnerable human being who'd been through hell and emerged scarred and tainted, but not wholly lost. As Zenna's hand crept into his, his fingers clenched and gripped it tight.

Lovick watched them. "And your stepmother?"

Max jerked his head in the direction of the desk. "She brought that thing back with her hoping for results, but as far as I know it never worked, her only real weapon was her own will-power."

"But it works for you?"

"It would—if I'd let it. But don't kid yourself, I'm not going to, you won't fool me twice."

"Even if it told you how she was murdered?"

"I don't give a damn how she was murdered. Good riddance to stinking rubbish, that's my epitaph for her, and I've changed my mind about keeping the flat. Clear her stuff out and burn the lot, I wouldn't touch it now for a million pounds. And if you want my advice—" his pale sick-looking eyes flickered briefly to the devil-carving and closed for a tight moment on remembered horror— "you'll burn that too. If you can."

"If I can?"

"If it'll let you. Come on, Zenna, we're going home."

But he wasn't allowed to leave quite so summarily. Lovick was still short on facts. "What brought you to these parts?" he demanded.

"Drifted," said Max briefly. "Job to job. After dad's death I was on my own. I was born here, if that counts. Meeting Zenna made me a fixture."

"And your stepmother?"

"Bumped into her one day in the market. Didn't even know she'd moved to Norwich. What she really wanted was a place in Wrexley where her friends were. One friend in particular—no, not a man, she wasn't thinking of marriage then. A Miss Turner or Turnham or—"

"Turnberry?"

"Could be. I wasn't interested."

Which may have been the biggest mistake of your life, thought Lovick suddenly. He'd just pinned down that elusive impression of familiarity. Miss Turnberry! Shave off this bloke's whiskers and add twenty years or so and they'd be the dead spit of each other. And this bloke was minus a mother. If the idea wasn't so plumb ridiculous he'd say—

But was it so ridiculous? Miss Turnberry had had a youth like everybody else. Forty years ago, she might even have been pretty, and if a travelling hardware man, say, had chanced to come her way—

That's it, thought Lovick with conviction. And Mrs. Sibley had hugged the secret to herself until it had suited her to track down her husband's ex-mistress and have fun. Miss Turnberry was a spinster of the old school, a pillar of the church and all that with her fancy dolls and Bring-and-Buys; the mere threat of exposure would have terrified her. Miss Purdy had said there was something queer about their friendship—'unhealthy' was the word she'd used; one woman domineering over the other and the other cringingly anxious to please her. Emotional blackmail. Was that how Mrs. S. had bought her way into the respectable Antiquarian Society and proceeded to corrupt a sizable bunch of 'em? Lovick was aware that he was leaping ahead of established fact but it fitted—it fitted. And it looked as though she'd been planning to draw Max and Zenna into the net—or maybe it was her sense of fun again, bringing Max to live within a hand's-breadth of his true mother and watching in the wings with malicious glee to see what happened . . .

Another thought jolted him. If that last bit was true, Miss Turnberry herself had had an overwhelming motive to shut her up for good and all. Not that she could have flown a helicopter, of course, but she could easily have given her the preliminary whack on the head which had made the rest possible—granting she was a member of the coven and others had been willing to help.

Max stirred restlessly. "Look, it's nearly lunch-time. When can we—"

"In a minute. Did you ever meet Miss Turnberry?"

"No, I told you, we never met any of Sibyl's friends."

"Suzi Barlow?"

"Who's she?"

Rumours of Suzi's death were already sweeping the town, but it was obvious they hadn't reached this couple. The blank stares on both faces were genuine. Lovick pressed again for some clue to the identity of Mrs. Sibley's intended bridegroom but came up against the same blank wall, and finally he let them go after reminding them that the inquest would be held tomorrow.

All he was left with was a list of the half dozen people who (Max claimed) would support his alibi for Tuesday night.

CHAPTER ELEVEN

Where in heck was Saunders? Must be nearly an hour since he'd gone chasing out after Bill Breck to bring him in before he could do himself or his ex-partner a mischief. Since then nobody had seen hide nor hair of him. Cocker too, thought Lovick peevishly. Why did everybody keep disappearing when he himself was up to his eyes in it? Fat lot of chance there was of getting home to his own lunch. He rang up his missus to tell her so, sent down to the canteen for sandwiches and coffee, sent down again (with a blistering comment) for mustard, and finally began to eat and brood.

The thing really sticking in his throat (apart from a lump of gristle which he threw in the waste-paper basket) was this business of the old witch contemplating marriage. What man in his right senses would want to take on a fat malicious old harridan who—

But that was just the point, of course. He wasn't in his right senses or he wouldn't have been at St. Edred's on Tuesday evening—that is, assuming he was one of the coven, which was so near a certainty in Lovick's mind that he refused for the moment to consider anything else.

Of course there was another possibility—that the desire had been all on her side and the wedding a matter of wishful thinking. What he'd heard of her, once she'd set her sights on a chap he wouldn't have stood a chance, and if he'd already happened to have a sweetie of his own—

Motive for murder there all right, especially as she

150

hadn't been above a bit of emotional blackmail. If the only way out of her clutches had been a bonk on the head—

If, if, if.

Establish his identity, Lovick thought, and the rest will click into place.

All right, then, who was he?

Somebody of standing or she wouldn't have looked at him twice. Somebody belonging to the Antiquarian Society. Somebody, in all probability, with an interest in Witchwater, too. And who fitted that bill? Obviously the three men most concerned in rebuilding the cottage to exact specifications. Begbie, who'd found the missing heir; Dillinger, who'd been responsible for the construction; and that old goat Wetherby who'd probably dug up the relevant details from his moth-eaten stock. And of the three he was inclined to pick Harvey Dillinger. Begbie, whatever his spare-time pursuits, still had some shreds of dignity and decency left; Wetherby was a dried-up little stick insect unlikely to appeal to a powerful full-blooded Black Widow spider; whereas Dillinger was a prosperous good looking widower of approximately her own age, inclined to fleshiness but she could hardly throw stones at him on that account; trendy enough to flatter her vanity and popular enough in local circles to make him a genuine catch. Most significant of all, in view of Max Sibley's disclosures, was the fact that he'd been courting Suzi Barlow, who'd undoubtedly been ' dealt with '.

Lovick stopped eating for a few moments and sat very still. Had Mrs. S., by spells or otherwise, set in train a movement to eliminate her young rival and actually succeeded, though too late to do herself any good? And had her own death been a futile attempt on Dillinger's part to forestall the coming tragedy and—

Lovick gave himself a shake. Dammit, he'd been within

an ace of assuming that witchcraft really worked. How could anyone induce a ruddy great cat to jump up at a girl and savage her twenty-four hours later? He must be round the twist.

And why didn't anyone cure decent ham any more? This lot tasted like anaemic blotting-paper. Pushing the plate away, he downed the rest of his coffee at a gulp and reached out a finger to the buzzer. High time Mr. Harvey Dillinger was politely invited to come round to the station and answer a few questions.

With the hole in the ceiling for starters.

* * *

While Superintendent Vallance was making a couple of unimportant private calls in Wrexley in order to put off his duty call on the major as long as possible, Sergeant Donzell was standing in front of his full-length bedroom mirror, completely satisfied with what he saw there. Buttons and boots and hat-badge reflected the precise amount of sparkle efficiency demanded. He'd had a haircut only yesterday and his sandy moustache, too, was neatly trimmed. Nothing to be done about his freckles, but since freckles weren't mentioned in regulations he was entitled to feel they didn't count.

This, he knew in his bones, was his finest hour. Lovick had explicitly stated that the Super would be calling here any minute. Well, what he'd actually said was ' Don't let him catch you asleep ', but it came to the same thing. Only natural the super would want to hear at first-hand exactly what the local sergeant had accomplished.

The local sergeant mentally reviewed his recent achievements with pride. Thanks to his resource in calling on the services of Major Barlow for transport, he'd reached the original trouble-spot of St. Edred's with the minimum of delay. Unofficial services, perhaps, but amply justified by the major's quick-witted discovery of the cock's provenance. Here again, following up this information, Donzell had acted promptly and efficiently, identifying the thieves that same evening. (Well, better not say 'thieves' with Suzi Barlow involved. Innocent child led astray by wicked influences? Or was that coming it too strong? Wiser to play it by ear.) Anyhow, whatever Lovick chose to say about the fact that he'd been fast asleep while the helicopter was ferrying passengers to and from St. Edred's, nobody could deny that he'd found the witch's body entirely on his own. He preened himself a little at this point. Quite true he'd found it more or less by accident (trust Lovick to make the most of that) but if he hadn't had the forethought, the intelligence, the devotion to duty to plan an all-night observation on the ruins, and furthermore the sagacity, the caution, the selflessness to take a roundabout route to reach them, she wouldn't have been found for weeks, maybe, as he was certainly entitled to point out to the Super in case it had escaped his attention. What else—

Oh yes, the business of the shoes, which he considered one of his best bits of detection to date. But there again he'd have to go carefully, depending on the exact quality of the friendship between the Super and Major Barlow. Tricky question, that. Until he was sure how the land lay, he must remember to speak of the major with affection and respect. And the girl, of course.

One thing he could state categorically: apart from Suzi, who'd brought her wicked ways with her from London, there were no devil-worshippers on his patch. He knew his flock too well for that. Witchcraft and such, including lewd naked frolics on the marshes, were wicked and unwelcome invasions from outside.

Giving a final tug to his tunic, he went through to his

front-room office, and here again—after a flick of his handkerchief over the chair-seat—he found nothing to cavil at. Book shelves, filing cabinets, desk and all were as neat and well arranged as the inside of a computer. Compared with Lovick's office, for instance, which he privately considered a dingy and unsightly mess, this was a model of bachelor efficiency, everything to hand and not an inch of wasted space, working-quarters to be proud of. He hoped the Super would agree with him.

He looked at his watch. Fifteen-minute drive at most from Wrexley. Knowing nothing of the Super's delaying tactics, he began to feel it was time he arrived. Flexing knees and fingers, he stationed himself by the window to keep watch and savour his coming triumph. Everything was in his favour, he thought smugly—Lovick nearing retirement, himself due for promotion, a tricky case being well handled at this end and Superintendent Vallance all to himself, ready to be impressed. Lovick might scoff at his gardening efforts but even these had their place. It all helped the image. Look at those daffodil-crammed borders —Percy Thrower himself couldn't better such an array. Not a weed among 'em. Edges straight as a die, whatever a die was; lawn freshly mown and not a dead leaf or worm-cast in sight. Bungalow walls freshly Snow-cemmed too—white—a D.I.Y. job back in February—and looking a fair treat. Even Lovick on his last visit had commented favourably on the green paintwork. Well, what he'd actually said was ' Done it to match your eyes, I see,' meant as a sour sort of joke, but Donzell knew jealousy when he saw it and hadn't let it disturb his pride in the job. Pity today's wasn't a social call, he could hardly take the Super round to the back to show him the D.I.Y. greenhouse and the—

He glanced at his watch again, a faint touch of anxiety beginning to cloud his complacency. Coffee was percolat-

154

ing in the kitchen and beer waiting in the fridge for the Super's use if and as required, but unless he appeared soon his errand would take him on to lunch-time—and then what? He could hardly depend on the sorrowing major for a meal and Norwich was all of eight miles further on. Would he expect—accept—be grateful for—

Hastily Donzell ran his mind over the contents of his larder. Tinned soup—that was okay. Cream of tomato, perhaps—no, the celery sounded better. Main course—no trouble there. Mrs. Jones next door who 'did' for him twice a week had dropped in after breakfast with a nice rabbit pie for his supper. He'd often suspected Zeke Jones of poaching and naturally he wouldn't have accepted it if there'd been the slightest suspicion of—but anyone could catch a rabbit on the heath and he'd had no qualms whatever in welcoming it. Good thing too, as it turned out; lettuce and tomatoes from the greenhouse and a jar of pickled onions and you had a feast for a king, let alone a Super, and no need to tell him he hadn't made the pastry himself. For afters, fruit salad, perhaps, three of his varied stock tipped out into the same dish—no, four, he'd add that special tin of lychees for good measure. He'd never tried it and this was a good excuse, bound to add class and flavour seeing they were so expensive. And a tin of cream, of course, to go with 'em. Sherry—beer—invalid port—

He breathed again. Efficiency vindicated. Everything under control. Ready for any emergency. That is, if—

Yes, yes, no need to panic. The laundry had delivered the clean tablecloth last week.

Funny the Super was taking so long, though. Surely he wouldn't have gone straight to the Hall, by-passing his local sergeant altogether? Unless that swine Lovick—

For a few moments Donzell saw red, suddenly convinced that Lovick, out of pure spite and jealousy, had talked him into doing just that, but his blood pressure subsided to normal as he realised that Lovick wouldn't have mentioned the visit at all if he'd felt like that. There still remained the possibility, however, that Vallance had driven straight to the Hall off his own bat, and Donzell spent the next few minutes teetering on the brink of uncertainty, unable to decide between streaking off to the Hall himself and catching him there, and giving him another ten minutes, say, to make sure he wouldn't turn up here directly his back was turned.

The phone settled the matter.

Leaping to it, he snatched up the receiver and was annoyed to find his voice coming out a semitone higher than usual. "Lindham Police. Sergeant Donzell speaking."

At first he couldn't make out what the bloke at the other end was saying. His own mind was slightly flustered but that was nothing to the agitation hitting him in reverse. All he knew for certain was that the speaker wasn't Superintendent Vallance. Finally he managed to establish that he was Major Barlow's handyman-gardener, an asthmatic old dodderer who obstinately refused to change his methods of pruning in spite of repeated attempts on Donzell's part to teach him better.

"Stop dithering, Biggs!" he ordered crisply as soon as this knowledge had sunk in. "Take a deep breath, man, and pull yourself together. Now, what is it? Be quick because I'm expecting an important visitor. Well?"

"The Major, Sarge—"

"What about him?"

"He's bin at the Scotch all mornin' an' I can't do nothin' with him, fust cryin' his heart out an' now ravin' like a blessed lunatic. Listen, can't you hear him? Smashin' up the furniture an'—oh, my gosh! That's the Persian vase gone! Drunk as a bleedin' lord."

Muffled banging and shouting did indeed form background effects to the old man's anguished wail, and Donzell's heart missed a beat. If the Super walked in on a scene like that—

Nothing for it but to get there himself and restore order. In double-quick time too—that last crash had sounded like a window. In a matter of seconds he was on his motor-bike speeding through the country lanes to the major's eighteenth-century residence on the fringe of Bilby Heath. No sign of the Super's car, thank heaven, and within four minutes he was flinging himself from his machine in front of the main steps and dashing up to the stout oak door.

Not stopping even to knock, he pushed it open and ran inside, pausing in the flagstoned hall for a moment to get his bearings. Half a moment was enough. From the library at the rear came an incoherent shout of rage followed by a couple of shots and indeterminate crashes, giving the impression that the whole place was falling about his ears. Plunging headlong into the centre of danger, he was conscious of only one thought. If the major was armed, he might never get to know what lychees tasted like after all.

* * *

Meanwhile, P.C. Saunders too was having his troubles. Wetherby's bookshop in the High Street was two doors below the butcher's over which Miss Turnberry lived. Unaware of this basic fact, he checked himself in the act of entering, staring in astonishment as Miss Purdy came running out of the butcher's and bolted past him in blind panic. A shade quicker on the uptake and he could have stopped her, but by the time he'd finished wondering how buying a couple of chops or half a pound of liver could have scared her silly, she was halfway to the bottom of the High Street. Making for the nick and old Mind-me-corns, he concluded, and dismissed her from his mind in favour of more important matters like catching up with Bill Breck before he blew a valve.

Wetherby's long, narrow shop was empty except for a couple of chattering and rather scared-looking sales-girls. His arrival was greeted with a squeal of excitement.

" Oooh, look, a copper ! Now's our chance, Sandra, I'm going to tell him."

" Watch what you're saying, Lucy ! The boss won't like—"

" Then he shouldn't run off and leave us here alone. Suppose that man comes back? And don't forget he's got a knife now. He might decide to wait for them and—"

" Knife ?" interrupted Saunders sharply.

" That's right, and I don't care what anybody says, he's *crazy*, the way he came rushing into the shop shouting ' Where's that bloody Dillinger?' with his eyes rolling and—"

" Don't exaggerate !" interjected the older girl. " It was only Bill Breck, I've known him donkey's years and he's as sane as you or me."

" He was out to get Dillinger, wasn't he?"

" Doesn't mean he wants to murder him."

" Then what did he want the knife for? Snatching it off the kitchen table and chasing through the whole house—even Mr. Wetherby's bedroom—swearing he'd find him and cut his heart out. If you ask me, Constable, it's a miracle those steps aren't running with blood !" Turning, she pointed a dramatic finger at a glass-panelled door raised a couple of steps at the back of the shop. " The boss and Mr. Dillinger were in there, see? It's Mr. Wetherby's private room—we call it the squint-hole, Sandra and me, because when we're climbing up the ladders—"

" Lucy!"

" Oh, don't be so stuffy! Everybody knows what old Wetherby's like. And it doesn't stop at looking either. If he pinches my bottom one more time—"

" You'll take it and come back for more, so shut up!"

Lucy pouted, and Saunders eyed the door again. Though partly screened by nylon net the glass panels allowed a good view down the length of the passages between the bookshelves. Squint-hole's right, he thought—nice and handy for watching potential book-pinchers and the mini-skirted legs of the two girls as they climbed up to reach the higher shelves.

Lucy took up her tale again. " What he forgets is, it works both ways. Up there we can see over the top of the net and we always know when he's got a 'special' customer. You know, for the books he doesn't let us see." She giggled. " Though between you and me—"

" Yes, yes," said Saunders hastily. He was willing to wager the kids got a kick out of looking at 'forbidden' books and rather envied them the chance, but that was neither here nor there. " Let's get this straight. Are you saying Mr. Dillinger's one of his 'specials'?"

" Well, that's the funny thing, it's what he usually comes for but there wasn't the sign of a book this morning. I was up the ladder having an eyeful, see? And old Dillinger looked queer enough, waving his arms and doing all the talking, but the poor old boss—honestly, he sat there all crumpled up like and I thought he was going to be sick. If you'd seen his face—"

" What about Breck?"

" Well, that's when it happened, see? All of a sudden he came bursting into the shop shouting—"

" Yes, I know what he was shouting."

" And Sandra was busy with a sale so I had to come down and talk to him. And honestly, he nearly went for

159

me, just because I said the boss was engaged. Well, it was true, wasn't it? The boss was engaged. But Mr. Breck—"

" Where is he now?"

" How should I know? And I wish you'd let me finish. How can I tell you if you keep interrupting? Anyway I was really scared by then so I said all right, I'll tell him he's wanted, but he just pushed past and was up those steps before I—and you won't believe this bit but every word of it's true, the room was absolutely empty! I couldn't believe it at first, I'd seen them from the ladder only a minute before, and what with all this talk of witch-craft about—well, I said to Sandra, it's just as if they'd vanished in a puff of smoke!"

" Or nipped up the stairs," said Saunders more prac-tically.

" Oh no, because Mr. Breck snatched up this knife and went all over the house looking for them—behind chairs, in cupboards and everything. You've no right, I said—didn't I, Sandra? But he kept pushing me out of the way and swearing and—"

" You, miss—" Saunders looked at Sandra—" there's a back door, I take it?"

" Of course there is and that's the way they went as soon as the shouting started. Why Lucy has to dress it all up—"

" Where would they make for?"

" Their lawyer's, most likely."

" And that was me, too," said Lucy, triumphantly. " Mr. Breck asked that and I said straight out, ' I know where *I'd* be if you came tearing into my house like a cyclone and poking about all over, and that's round at my lawyer's, double-quick, taking out a conjunction,' and he sort of clapped his hand to his head—like this—" her gesture was graphic—" and said ' Begbie! He's another of 'em!' and was off before I could say—"

" Thanks."

Saunders was off, too, before she could say whatever silly thing came into her head next. Why in heck she couldn't have told him in the first place—

Lucky it wasn't far. Begbie's offices occupied the two bottom floors of a nice old house in a side road off the middle of the High Street. Lived over 'em with his wife, Saunders recollected, and was rather surprised to see the place looking as dignified and intact as usual when he came in sight of it. Subconsciously he'd expected it to look like the victim of a bomb outrage, more or less. As soon as he got near, however, he heard definite sounds of trouble on the first floor. Downstairs, in the reception office, two frightened typists were clinging to each other behind a desk, their eyes fixed on the ceiling as though expecting it to fall down at any moment, and sundry bumps and thuds up there seemed to bear out this expectation, to say nothing of a scattering of powdered plaster over papers and filing cards. One of the girls pointed speechlessly to the stairs. Saunders took these three at a time, emerging on to a narrow landing with a plentiful choice of doors. Teetering for a second to get his bearings, he changed course and dived straight for the one where the noise was coming from, flinging it open on a scene of chaos.

Mr. Begbie's office looked as though a minor tornado had swept through it, reaping a harvest of loose papers and paperclips en route. Overturned chairs and an up-ended typewriter lay on the floor amid a welter of scattered lawbooks, and the room was full of the smell of scorching leather. It was also full of people. In one corner a frightened little woman (who could only be Mrs. Begbie) had a hand pressed to her mouth in voiceless panic; her stout, silver-haired husband stood over by the window clutching a telephone and chattering into it like a demented monkey; from behind a big leather-covered armchair peered the agonised, wrinkled little face of Angus Wetherby, bobbing back every few seconds in terror when the flow of violence threatened to engulf him; while the middle of the stage was occupied by Breck and Dillinger, locked together in a blind struggle of hate. The knife lay forgotten on the floor. Cannoning into furniture, tripping over debris, each man was intent on getting a stranglehold on the other. Dillinger, out of condition, was panting and sweating heavily, and in spite of his size was beginning to get the worst of it when Saunders' arrival gave him the fraction of a second's advantage. Facing the door, he saw him first and was able to absorb the shock that much sooner. Wrenching free during the moment of distraction, he caught up a chair, swung it over his head and lashed forward at his opponent.

The result was catastrophic. Mrs. Begbie screamed, Begbie dropped the telephone, Wetherby popped back out of sight completely and Breck ducked. The descending chair knocked Saunders' helmet off and caught him a powerful blow on the side of the head, folding him on the floor in a world of stars and blackness.

Downstairs, the ceiling scattered fresh plaster and the two typists screamed in unison.

* * *

Lovick did something he hadn't done before during more than thirty years on the Force. He fell asleep at his desk.

Well, not fell asleep. Dozed off for a few seconds, more like it. All right, a few minutes. Half an hour at most. What else would you expect after traipsing over half Norfolk and being up practically all night working?

He sat up rubbing his eyes and glaring at the clock as if it had bitten him. What had he been doing when—

Oh yes, these ruddy reports. No, wait a minute. Something more urgent. He took a drink of water to cool his parched throat. Something more urgent—but what? He sat back and closed his eyes. Start at the beginning. St. Edred's. Witch falling off a broomstick. Girl mauled by cat. Miss Purdy—

Miss Purdy came into it somewhere, she always did, but for the life of him he couldn't think—oh, of course. Hole in the ceiling. Dillinger. Bill Breck and his blessed screwdriver. Saunders and—

His back straightened with a jerk. Saunders!

He jabbed a finger towards the buzzer but the telephone beat him to it. He snatched up the receiver instead. " Lovick here."

Donzell. And that was another—

Spluttering, too. What the hell was the matter with everybody?

" S-s-sir! The major—Major Barlow—"

" You don't have to spell his name, man. Super there yet?"

" No, sir."

" Well, go on. What is it?"

" The major, sir. He's drunk."

" In charge of a car?"

" No, sir, but—"

" Disturbing the peace?"

" You could call it that, sir," said Donzell, sibilants quenched by sheer gritting of his teeth. " He's just put a couple of shots through his library ceiling. We managed to get the shotgun away from him—the gardener and I— and entice him up to his bedroom, but he resisted all efforts to get him into bed and finally I locked the door on him and phoned his doctor. He seemed quiet enough then, sir—"

" Got another bottle of booze up there," Lovick diagnosed accurately.

163

" Could be, sir. Of course, if I'd known that—"

" Dammit, if I can smell his breath from here—"

" He seemed perfectly reasonable, sir, or I shouldn't have left him, but now he's working himself into another lather—shouting and banging—maybe you can hear him—"

" I didn't think it was your heart thumping."

" No, sir." The humourless sergeant clenched his teeth again; never had Lovick seemed so hard to bear. " I think he's genuinely over the edge, sir, and his doctor's out on a maternity case, so if you could send Grant—or any other medico—" He broke off with as desperate an expletive as his Presbyterian upbringing would allow. " Oh, cripes! He's broken another window! Sir, I'd better get back to him—no, wait—"

Somebody's voice (the gardener's, presumably) had become raised in an anguished howl sending a shock-wave rippling round Lovick's eardrum. " Mr. Donzell, sir! Quick! He's busted the window an' climbin' down the ivy! I won't be able to hold him—oh, my gawd!" There was a muffled crash in the distance.

Donzell, with a clear view of the catastrophe through an open french window, promptly broke into a running commentary. " Sir, he's landed on him! They're fighting. Major's on top and pummelling him hard. Biggs is—"

" Get out and stop him, man!"

But Donzell was in full spate. " He's up—he's streaking for—sir, the helicopter! I'll have to ring off and stop him."

" What gave you that idea?"

The receiver slammed down.

Lovick followed suit, thinking rapidly. Either Donzell was chasing a fleeing murderer, or drink and grief between them had smashed the old man's wits. In that case, what was he after, suicide or revenge? Revenge, most likely—

revenge on the thing responsible for his grand-daughter's death, that blasted cat. That's why he needed the chopper. Weak heart or not, he could probably make it as far as Witchwater, and once there—

Donzell had the shotgun but, for all any of 'em knew, the major kept an arsenal up in his bedroom in case of burglars and could still be armed. The cat might be improved by a bullet inside him, but a raving lunatic with a loaded gun was another matter, especially with a pregnant girl concerned. Maybe Ken Daw could talk sense into him and maybe not. No way of warning 'em since Witchwater wasn't on the phone. Of course, with any luck Donzell would stop him reaching the helicopter, but—

Cursing under his breath, Lovick snatched up his uniform cap and plunged outside, pulling up short at the sight of Ken Daw himself arguing with the desk sergeant.

" What the devil are you doing here?" he demanded.

P.C. Cocker stepped forward smartly. " You told me to fetch him, sir."

" *I* did? But that—" He checked himself, remembering that some time back in the recesses of the morning he'd done that very thing.

Ken said belligerently : " And I want to know why I've been hauled here and—"

" Never mind that. Where's your wife?"

" Margery? Back home, of course."

" Alone?"

" Of course she's alone. Why in hell—"

" How did you get here?"

" What's that got to do with—"

" Cocker?"

" Motorboat, sir. Moored at the staithe."

" Come along, then, quick. Stebbings, get through to Doc. and send him after us. Tell him Witchwater—in a hurry. Barlow's sick and on the warpath, may need an ambulance. Keep in touch with his house, though—Donzell may need help. Daw, is he capable of flying that chopper?"

Ken said dazedly: "He's been warned not to, but—"

"Come on. The boat."

CHAPTER TWELVE

Miss Purdy had made the same journey twenty minutes earlier.

As P.C. Saunders had surmised, her first objective in that headlong flight from Miss Turnberry's flat had been the police station and Inspector Lovick, but before reaching it she'd changed her mind. By now Miss Turnberry would know she'd been rumbled. The flight alone would have told her, and one glance at her rifled worktable and piece-box would have confirmed it, though fortunately she didn't know about the damning 'Suzi' doll which had been delivered by hand.

So what next? Her instant reaction must have been to speed things up. She'd already made clear her intention to invade Witchwater, and Miss Purdy hadn't the slightest doubt that once inside the cottage her takeover would be total. Unsuspecting and hospitable, Margery with her unborn child stood in horrifying danger and she must be got away at once—now—immediately—before her aunt could reach her. How Miss Turnberry would get there—broomstick?—was beyond Miss Purdy's control, but she had to beat her somehow. Every second counted. There was no time for Lovick, no time either for a trek over the marshes even if she'd been able to cope with it physically. A boat—a motorboat—was the only answer.

Although she'd never owned a motor-cruiser she knew how to handle one; knew too that the hotel at the bottom of the High Street kept two or three small cabin-cruisers tuned and ready for chance custom even this early in the season. Thankfully, being well known there, she was able to hire *Mermaid* with the minimum of fuss and delay.

The fine weather had brought out more boats than she'd expected but she was able to make good speed down-river, keeping an anxious lookout for the insignificant creek on the left which would take her to Witchwater Broad. When last she'd been this way, the entrance had been all but concealed by hanging willow fronds and encroaching rushes, but she'd forgotten the cottage had been rebuilt since then and Ken's motorboat needed almost daily access. Trees had been trimmed back and a channel cleared and the 'PRIVATE' board newly painted. The creek itself was narrow and winding, demanding all her attention to avoid running aground or fouling the propeller, but it wasn't much more than two hundred yards long and after a few nerve-taxing minutes she emerged into open water with a striking view of the cottage on the opposite bank, picturesque and innocent-looking against its background of budding alders.

Keeping to the line of channel-posts marking cleared water, she steered for the landing stage jutting out from the grass bank, tying up there with a wary eye for possible danger. No sign of Elimauzer, though, or—thank heaven—of Miss Turnberry. The only things to protest at her coming were a family of moorhens which scuttled away, half-paddling and half flying, as she cut the engine. The absence of Ken's boat was disturbing, and but for the thin blue feather of smoke rising from the chimney she might have thought Margery was out too and felt all the panic of being without human contact. This might still be true. Her first knock brought no answer. Stepping back and glancing upwards, she saw a curtain twitch behind the latticed panes and waved urgently. A few moments later the door opened and the girl almost fell into her arms.

"Oh, Miss Purdy! Thank goodness you've come, I've been *praying* for someone to—"

"Are you alone?"

"Yes, that's why I'm so scared, a copper's taken Ken to the police station—for questioning, he said, but—"

"Where's the cat?"

"Locked in the spare room, the policeman did that and told me not to let him out, but he hasn't had any food or—just listen to him scratching the door and howling—"

"Leave him alone, he's quite safe, it's you I'm worried about. We've got to get away at once."

"But I can't just leave—"

"You've got to, believe me it's vital. How long will it take you to pack an overnight bag?"

"But why—"

"Oh, please don't argue! Just do as I say."

Almost pushing her upstairs, she watched her flinging a few clothes into a suitcase, urging her on when precious seconds were lost in hesitation. "It doesn't matter what you take. Just enough to tide you over."

"Will Ken be coming back?"

"I don't know. We'll be seeing him in Wrexley. Oh, what's the matter now?"

"My toothbrush." Margery pounced towards the old-fashioned washstand with its china jug and bowl, galling substitutes for a bathroom in this day and age. "Where am I going to stay?"

"With me—anywhere—we'll discuss that later. Surely you don't need—"

"I've finished." The case was snapped and locked. Across the scrap of landing Elimauzer screamed and hurled himself at the locked door with renewed fury. Shuddering, Margery gave a last look round and then, unexpectedly, uttered a little cry of relief and dropped the bag back on the bed. "Oh, look, there's Aunt Agnes! If she'll stay with me I won't mind so much. Let's wait till—"

"No!" Snatching up the bag, Miss Purdy took her by the arm and fairly ran her downstairs. "She mustn't find you here. She's ill—dangerous—not herself—I can't stop to explain, you must take my word for it—"

Oh, why had the fool of a girl dallied so long? Miss Purdy too had seen through the window Miss Turnberry's scraggy, gangling figure emerge from the alders at a loping run. Less than a minute's breathing space—and Margery still holding back to argue—

"Ill—dangerous—what do you mean? She looked all right to me."

"For heaven's sake, Margery—"

"Anyway, she'll see us. We can't go out now."

"The back way—hurry—" But in the kitchen doorway Miss Purdy came to a sudden stop, breathing an urgent: "Quiet!" Miss Turnberry had halted underneath the spare-room window and was looking upwards, a fatuous expression on her bony face. Through the open front door her twittering voice reached them clearly.

"Elimauzer! *Dear* pussy! Come to Auntie, then!" The crooning silliness of the invitation sent shivers down Miss Purdy's spine.

Margery whispered urgently: "I've just remembered, that window catch is loose. If he tries to jump—"

And that was exactly what he did. There was a tinkle of breaking glass as the casement banged back against the wall, then the soft thud of his landing and an exultant cry of: "Clever pussy!" But 'clever pussy' didn't act according to plan. Instead of 'coming to Auntie' he backed away with every hair on his back bristling and then, with a mew of pure terror, bolted back into the cottage and streaked towards the kitchen as if for sanctuary.

His panic was infectious. Margery gasped with fright and was first out into the back yard, leaving Miss Purdy

170

to shut the door and bar his way. Together they raced round the side of the cottage and across the bank, missing Miss Turnberry by seconds. She was inside the cottage, calling distantly, before they reached the boat.

Torn between fear of the cat and concern for her, Margery stumbled and would have stopped if Miss Purdy hadn't propelled her onwards and almost pushed her aboard the cruiser.

" Quick! Untie us while I start the engine."

" But Aunt Agnes—she's calling me—"

" For pity's sake! Do as you're told."

Turning space was limited and *Mermaid* was built for holiday comfort rather than speed or manoeuvrability. In her haste to get away Miss Purdy collided with one channel-post and skeetered drunkenly past another before making headway; which at least had the merit of concentrating Margery's mind on keeping her balance instead of what was happening on-shore.

Then came the inevitable cry from the bank. " Margery! Come back! Come back! It's only me!" Flapping her arms wildly Miss Turnberry came loping over the grass, a gaunt grotesque figure in a loose drab raincoat with a bright blue scarf tied over her head. " Come back! You can't leave me here alone!"

Her voice rose to a scream. They were nearly halfway across the broad by now and for a moment it looked as though she was crazy enough to plunge in after them. Margery clutched Miss Purdy's sleeve. " She's right, we must go back—oh, please—"

" We're going for help. She needs a doctor."

" I don't believe it. How could she have walked all this way if she wasn't fit?"

" Margery!" There was certainly vigour enough in that screech to reach them across the rapidly-widening gap, but there was something more—a viciousness and fury that froze the words on the girl's tongue. "Margery! You silly stupid bitch! Come back at once or I'll—" The string of obscenities grew fainter but lingered on the air long after the reeds shut off the cottage from view.

Margery sat down, fighting back nausea. She couldn't believe it was Aunt Agnes standing there shaking her fists and screaming abuse after them—Aunt Agnes, who though old and silly and twittery had never spoken a really harsh word in her life. Of course they were behaving unforgivably in running out on her like this, but even so—

Miss Purdy was right, she must be ill, the shock of her friend's death had unhinged her. And yet—

It was all too much. She covered her face with her hands and began to cry.

Miss Purdy heard her but tried not to listen. It was her job to get them back to Wrexley as soon as possible. She wouldn't feel really safe until they were out of this narrow winding creek and on the open river. The blind bends taxed all her patience, the tall reeds hemming them in made her feel claustrophobic. Part of her mind was aware that the engine seemed to have developed an odd kind of echo, but far more distracting was the sound of a helicopter flying dangerously low overhead. As she glanced up apprehensively, a sudden shout in front warned her of a more imminent danger.

"Look out, there! Watch it!"

"Ken!" screamed Margery, on her feet at the same moment. The foreground, which had been mostly reeds, was now filled with the white bows of another cruiser bearing down on them.

Under the circumstances Miss Purdy did her best. Wrenching the wheel violently she succeeded in ramming *Mermaid*'s nose into a thicket of stems and mud. At the same moment she was knocked off her feet by a jarring shock on the boat's starboard side. Sitting up dazedly a few seconds later, she heard more shouting and saw the second boat tilted at a heady angle in the mud of the opposite bank, while the sight of a uniformed constable struggling in the water proved that her hazy memory of a loud splash hadn't been at fault.

Another boat, she thought bemusedly. Coming at us round the bend. That must have been what the 'echo' was. We met nearly head on. I was looking at that wretched helicopter and—

Oh dear! Inspector Lovick! He'll say it was all my fault.

As Lovick's enraged face appeared over the side of the tilted boat, capless and with a trickle of blood escaping from a cut forehead, he'd have said all that and a great deal more if the helicopter hadn't appeared above the reeds again hurtling straight towards the cottage. Miss Purdy was destined to dream about the resultant crash for years. The whole world seemed to explode in noise and screams and smoke, and again she did the only sensible thing under the circumstances.

She fainted.

* * *

"If you hadn't come blasting at us with that blessed boat—" Lovick began to inform her heatedly, but Ken Daw's interruption was immediate and fierce.

"Leave her alone! If she hadn't got Margery out in time—"

"All right, I grant she saved your wife's life, but I still say—"

"Must you, Inspector?" asked Miss Purdy wearily.

It was late that same evening in her own flat where Lovick, dead beat after a tiring and traumatic day, had dropped in for a final word and a nightcap, not surprised

173

to learn Margery was asleep in the spare room under sedatives. But for Miss Purdy's hospitality the young couple would have been homeless, since Major Barlow and his chopper had made a thorough job of destroying the cottage as well as themselves, the cat and Miss Turnberry. Using the machine as a battering ram, the major had crashed into the building at full speed, setting it on fire and reducing the remains to twisted metal, charred timbers and pulverised rubble. And so for the third time in its turbulent and unsavoury history Witchwater had gone up in smoke and ended in ashes, and Miss Purdy hoped devoutly that no twisted or perverted mind would contemplate setting one brick on top of another at that site again.

Miss Turnberry hadn't died immediately. Though badly crushed by debris she'd been outside the cottage at the moment of impact and had escaped the fire. It had been touch and go, however. Cocker (the constable who'd fallen overboard) had managed to push his way through the swampy reeds to dry ground and drag her clear from the inferno at the risk of his own life, and though barely conscious she had still been alive when Ken and Margery had reached her hard on Lovick's heels.

Margery had cradled the dying woman in her arms—no longer the evil blaspheming creature of Miss Purdy's special nightmare but the loving, pious aunt she'd known in childhood. The devil—if devil it was—had gone out of her. In that scarred and mortally broken body, she had been restored to herself.

" She smiled at me," Margery had whispered during the drive back to Wrexley. " Just as she used to when I was little. How *could* she have said those awful things in the boat?"

" My dear, she didn't." Miss Purdy's voice was soft with pity. " She wasn't herself then. Literally."

" You mean—Mrs. Sibley—but that's too fantastic. I

can't believe—"

"Why not? She dominated her in life. And last night, off-balance and suffering from shock, she must have found her an easy victim." Her breath caught. "I should know. It so very nearly happened with me."

"Then you do think she—Mrs. Sibley was a witch?"

"Not in the accepted sense." Miss Purdy's voice grew stronger. "I think she was a greedy, malicious, domineering woman with enormous will-power and an unlimited capacity for evil, but the sort of power she'd have sold her soul to possess was an illusion, or at least unattainable. When she couldn't get results by force of personality she was reduced to trickery or blackmail like any other pervert. Thank heaven she was beaten in the end and your poor aunt's soul was able to find peace."

It wasn't a theory she cared to propound to Lovick. As far as he was concerned, Miss Turnberry had unfortunately got caught in the holocaust on a routine visit to her niece. Miss Purdy hadn't shown him the two dolls from the dead woman's flat for fear he'd jump to the wrong conclusion. She was convinced they'd been fashioned under duress with no knowledge of their possible use. The grey-haired doll was already ashes in her kitchen-stove. The Suzi doll lay in a drawer of her desk because she might yet change her mind and tell him how it had dropped through the letter-box. After all, it couldn't hurt Miss Turnberry now; it could only incriminate the person who'd brought it.

Lovick sipped his whisky and eyed young Daw. "And now, my lad, let's have the truth about St. Edred's."

Ken lifted a haggard face. "I've already made a statement."

"As little as you could get away with. I want the rest. So unless you object to Miss Purdy hearing—"

Ken flushed. "It isn't that. It's—Margery."

"You haven't told her?"

"How can I, with the baby coming and all? I feel sick every time I think about it. Suzi—I didn't even like the damned girl. I was flattered, I suppose, because she seemed to fancy me, but—do I have to go on?"

"Get it off your chest," advised Lovick, not unkindly.

"She spoke about this black magic stuff as though it was a big giggle. I don't know how seriously she really took it. I helped her catch the cockerel—you can't call it stealing, I slipped a fiver through the letterbox in payment. Did old Mother Pegg tell you that?"

"She may have told Donzell. She didn't tell me."

"Perhaps she didn't connect the two things. Anyway, back home Suzi slipped sleeping tablets into the old man's bedtime drink. We took off about ten and landed at St. Edred's. Suzi was covered up in a long black cloak and it wasn't till—well, later, I found she'd got nothing on underneath. About half a dozen others were there already, masks and hoods and all that. It was difficult to know who was who but I recognised—" He stopped suddenly. "Will they get into bad trouble?"

"Depends," said Lovick flatly.

"Depends on what?"

"How much they knew about Mrs. Sibley's death."

"Dillinger took the chopper up."

"He admits it, otherwise you wouldn't have got off so lightly yourself. Why didn't somebody tell me he's a qualified pilot?"

"I thought you knew. He was in the Fleet Air Arm with a painter called Stratton."

"I remember that now, he gave me a lift. What I'm saying is, nobody took the trouble to jog my memory earlier." Lovick sounded aggrieved. What did people think he was, a ruddy computer? He caught Miss Purdy's eye and decided not to labour the point. Instead he continued: "Dillinger's in custody, of course, but so far all I've got for what happened in the abbey is his unsupported story. Wetherby's taken an overdose of something or other and can't be questioned till they've finished Hoovering his inside. The rest of the mob's sitting tight, we'll get round to 'em in time but I need help now, so what about it?"

Ken drew a long breath. " I don't know what happened in the abbey. First I knew was when the engine started up. By the time we got there he'd taken off and the rest of the lousy pack was scarpering like flies, making for whatever they'd come in—cars, boats, broomsticks for all I know. Not one of 'em stopped to help or give us any information." His tone was bitter. " All they cared about was keeping their bloody names out of the papers. Suzi was sweating too—she'd got her mask on again by then—"

" How come you weren't with the rest of them at the time?"

Ken flushed again. " We were taking a walk."

" So you said at the station. Let's have the truth."

" All right, what *do* you do with a naked bird? I didn't plan it that way. I'd stuck by the helicopter, told her straight out I wasn't going to strip or join in the fun or do anything whatever except wait to take her home. But she eased out of the ceremonies pretty early and suggested we go for a walk instead. The chanting and some putrid incense were getting on my wick by then, so I agreed, but we didn't go far, just round the other side of the ruins and found a dry spot to sit on. And then—well—"

" Next thing you heard was the helicopter."

" Next thing I took an interest in, anyway. After about half an hour or so." He cast a half-defiant, half-shamefaced glance at Miss Purdy, who was sitting up very straight. " Sorry, I sound like a louse, shoving all the blame on a dead girl, and I'd *feel* like one if she hadn't *meant* it to happen, right from the start. I know that now and I suppose I knew it then, but it didn't seem to matter. That hellish chanting was still going on and—the whole atmosphere—I can't describe it—all I know is I was a damned fool and if Margery gets to hear of it she'll go crackers. That's why I hope you'll both have the decency to call it— just a walk."

Lovick looked at him in silence before saying pointedly : " Suzi was Dillinger's girl."

Ken was white now. " That's right."

" Did he know she was with you?"

" I can't see how. I mean—those masks and cloaks—"

" The coven was one short. He must have suspected—"

" That was Suzi's business, not mine. I didn't lure her away from him, if that's what you're getting at. She came out to me."

" You know Mrs. Sibley was planning to marry him?"

" Suzi did and it was one big laugh. That fat old cow had about as much chance as—"

" The fat old cow could count too."

" Meaning what?"

" She too knew the coven was one short, and what's more she found out why. According to Dillinger, they were all beginning to pair off and he was in a muck-sweat about Suzi when Mrs. S. flung her arms round his neck and told him what you were up to, slobbering something about herself being his true and only love and—"

Miss Purdy shuddered. " Don't!"

He admitted frankly it made him want to retch himself. " And as far as he was concerned it was the last straw. Seems she fell for him during the decorating upstairs and he'd been obliged to play along to a certain extent because she was footing the bill, but he swears there was never any mention of marriage. He had the devil's own job to shake her off. Admits he pushed a bit too hard and sent her flying but it was pure accident—he says—that she cracked her head on the ' altar ' in falling. We've had the blood analysed, by the way, and some of it's human and her blood group. The shock sobered him up, he claims he went through the motions of examining her and thought she was dead. So did everybody else, apparently, and the party began to break up in a hurry, all except Wetherby whom he grabbed before he could escape. The broomstick idea was Wetherby's, according to Dillinger, who was all for shoving her in the pool and scarpering himself, but Wetherby pointed out there was no time to clean up the place and anyhow the labour force was evaporating; he thought she'd make a useful red herring, turning our minds away from respectable citizens like builders and book-sellers and solicitors. Plenty of respectable people in the Antiquarians; he hoped to get lost in the crush. I'd say he's been reading too many of his own books."

Ken was looking sick. " I knew she was there, I'd recog-nised her voice at the beginning, but I took it for granted she'd sloped off with the rest of the pack. There was nothing to show—"

" Didn't you ask Dillinger why he went up?"

" Of course I did, I was waiting for him when he got back and blew my top, asked him what the devil he meant by touching the chopper at all. And he just looked at Suzi and said : ' Felt like it. Any objections?' and Suzi looked a bit queer and told me to shut up. And that was that. We were the only three left. We all went home."

" Without bothering to make sure your stories tallied."

" Neither Suzi nor I knew murder was involved."

" I'll accept that," said Lovick after a pause. " How about when you did know it? The next evening, for instance?"

" Just as I said, she phoned me at the pub and I told her to go to hell, but she said we'd got to get our stories straight and if I didn't meet her she'd come on to the cottage and bring Margery into it. You can see the jam I was in, especially as Margery didn't like being left on her own again. When it came to the point we had words about it, stood arguing on the doorstep, which was how that infernal cat got out."

"I'd like to be sure you didn't let it out on purpose."

Ken's chin jerked up. "I didn't. I can see what you're thinking, I had a damned good motive for wanting to shut her mouth, but how could I have known she'd get anything more than a fright which might have made her open it a ruddy sight wider? Besides, I'd already made up my mind, I was chucking the job in. I never wanted to come here in the first place and that cottage gave Margery the creeps, I knew she'd be glad to get out of it and the sooner the better. We're going back to Plymouth." He added savagely: "The air's cleaner down there."

"You didn't speak to Suzi on the marshes?"

"No, she was dead when I reached her and that's heaven's own truth."

"No need to bring heaven into it, it's the other place you should be worrying about. What about Witchwater?"

"Give it to the coots."

Lovick set his glass down. "Was Begbie one of the coven?"

"Could have been," said Ken guardedly, "but he's been pretty decent to me and Margery and I hope he's in the clear."

"Probably is. We've searched his place but he's had time to get rid of anything incriminating and there's no evidence either way. Dillinger and Wetherby flew into his wide open arms when they were cornered, but that may have been in the way of business. You'd better have a word with him. Your wife is probably Miss Turnberry's heir."

"Heir to what?"

"The flat, for one thing. She owned the freehold."

"You mean the one above the butcher's shop? I

wouldn't live there for any money. I'm not having my kid tainted with witchcraft."

" Up to you, of course, but there's another thing you should know. Miss Turnberry had a son."

" A—*son*?"

" In her far youth. By the late Mr. Sibley. Illegitimate, of course, as he proudly informed me. Slob of forty-odd, now living in Norwich. Doesn't know or care who his mother was. Seems he severed all ties from birth and the Sibleys brought him up. After all, bastards were bastards in those days and her father was a parson."

Miss Purdy said sharply: " But Mrs. Sibley knew her identity?"

" Oh yes. Either wormed it out of hubby when he was alive or found papers after his death."

" And she came to Norfolk on purpose to turn it to her own advantage."

" To put the screws on Miss Turnberry, yes, that's my guess too. Didn't need money, but a slave who couldn't answer back must have been useful in all sorts of ways. And Miss Turnberry couldn't answer back—not without having her lurid past exposed. Poor woman's life must have been hell, one long drag to avoid offending her."

" Did she know her son was living so close?"

" I very much doubt it. I think Mrs. Sibley was planning an interesting confrontation—for both of them— when she'd got him safely tucked up in the top flat."

" This," said Miss Purdy strongly, " is the most vicious thing yet. I know she liked playing around with people's lives, but—Kenneth, I hope you won't dream of telling Margery about this son of hers."

" Eh? Oh, of course not." Ken wasn't really interested in his aunt-in-law's forty-year-old peccadilloes. For a self-proclaimed enemy of capitalism he had a remarkably well-developed eye to the main chance. He said quite fiercely : " And if this bastard thinks he can come along and do Margery out of her rights——"

" He can't," said Lovick, " unless the old girl's specifically left something to him, which doesn't seem likely if she was trying to forget he existed. Miss Purdy's right, you'd better forget it too. I simply thought you ought to know, that's all."

Soon afterwards Ken muttered an excuse and said goodnight, looking the reverse of happy. In the doorway he turned for a final word with his hostess. " I haven't thanked you properly for saving Margery's life."

More than her life, thought Miss Purdy involuntarily, remembering the unborn child. Aloud she said : " My dear boy, I did no more than I had to."

" More than some people do. Don't worry, I'll make it up to her. About Suzi, I mean."

The door closed behind him. Lovick knocked his pipe out. " Suppose I'd better be getting along too. Tomorrow's another blessed day."

" Just a minute." On impulse she went over to the desk, took out the Suzi doll and laid it on the table in front of him. " This came through Miss Turnberry's letter-box while I was with her in her flat this morning."

Examining it, he looked up sharply. " By post?"

" No, by hand."

" What did she say about it?"

" I didn't show it to her."

" Did you see who——"

" No, but the butcher may have noticed who passed through the shop. My guess is Dillinger before Saunders got on his trail. It's pretty clear he was the man I heard in Mrs. Sibley's flat while the removal men were busy. He had to make sure she'd left nothing behind connecting him with witchcraft."

" Also to leave that screwdriver," commented Lovick

grimly. "He knew we'd find that cavity and tried to shove the blame on Breck."

In the stress of subsequent happenings Miss Purdy had forgotten Bill Breck. She said with sudden anxiety: "Did he catch up with him?"

"Oh yes, in Begbie's office. Begbie managed to babble for help and a squad car got there just in time to prevent murder."

"I hope Breck isn't under arrest."

"No. I doubt if Dillinger will charge him with assault, it'd mean his own dirty tricks coming out. Half Breck's business troubles were deliberately contrived by Dillinger and the rest was pure coincidence. Witchcraft!" He snorted. "Makes you sick, the way folks let 'emselves be taken in. None of the silly capers these fools got up to were the real thing. When they had any effect at all it was pure trickery. But this thing—" His voice changed as he turned the doll over and over, finally concentrating on the red ink 'scratches'. "This is something else. Where d'you reckon he got hold of it?"

"I think he found it in Mrs. Sibley's flat while he was going through it. The most likely possibility is that she forced Miss Turnberry to make it, then tried a private cursing ceremony of her own, driving a pin through the heart in the old way hoping it would work. If so, it's an irony of fate that it did work—but only after she was dead herself."

"You saying this needle in a doll caused the girl's death?"

"Who knows?" she replied soberly.

"I do!" he exploded. "And it ruddy well didn't! You'll be telling me next these imitation scratches caused the real thing. How in heck could she have known the flaming cat was going to be let out?"

"Did you find any red ink in her flat?"

"No, but——"

"I'll be surprised if there's none in Dillinger's office. If he took the doll from her flat on Wednesday morning he had it in his possession all night—and by the next morning he knew how Suzi had died. I think he drew those scratches himself to implicate Miss Turnberry."

"But why——"

"He was in a state where he had to hit out at somebody. And the doll was her work. That made her an accomplice. Putting it through her door was an act of revenge. He may even have planned an anonymous tip to send you there if the Breck business hadn't driven it out of his head."

Lovick rubbed his nose. Could be, of course. Dillinger could have pushed the thing through the letter-box on his way to the bookshop which was practically next door. A question to the butcher would probably settle it, though it wasn't really important now. Dillinger had enough to answer for without that, in the deliberate jettisoning of an unconscious woman.

"Have you traced the rest of the coven?" asked Miss Purdy.

"Give me time. Wetherby will cough when we're ready. Most of the masks and cloaks will have gone up in smoke by then but we'll know enough to make some of 'em pretty uncomfortable for a while."

"I'm glad the major was out of it."

"So am I," Lovick agreed unexpectedly. "Pompous old pest but he meant well and deserved a better granddaughter. And a better end." Turning to go, he thought of something else and cocked an eye upwards. "You going to let those flats again?"

"No," said Miss Purdy, promptly and firmly. "If Ken decides he doesn't want Miss Turnberry's—and I think he's wise to take Margery right away from here—I shall ask him to consider letting it to Shirley and David Carter. Mrs. Sibley's furniture will be placed in store for her stepson to deal with at his leisure. And then I shall put the house up for sale. I really don't wish to live here any more."

" Where will you go?"

" To my cottage in France. I don't think I'll ever come back to England. You and Mrs. Lovick will always be very welcome visitors, of course. No doubt," she added with a wry smile, " you'll be glad to see the back of me and my ' meddling '."

" Not at all," he said, and surprised himself by realising he meant it. " Due to retire myself pretty soon and we might even come and join you. So if you find a nice place to let near by—or even for sale if it doesn't cost the earth— I hope you'll let us know."

" Very willingly indeed, Inspector."

" Oh, come on, call me Albert."

It was the final accolade.

* * *

In Wrexley Cottage Hospital, two bandaged and slightly-concussed warriors eyed each other from adjacent beds.

Donzell's stiff lips moved first. " What put you here, Saunders?"

" Chair leg, Sarge. And you?"

Donzell's mind wrestled briefly with two distinct visions —one of heroic combat between himself and a demented major for control of the helicopter and the other of a slippery rug by the french window which had scuppered him before he could even leave the house. His Presbyterian conscience won.

He said, sourly but truthfully: " I ran into a door."

OUR RECORD OF PREVIOUS CRIMES

Some of the exciting tales of murder, mystery, danger, detection and suspense already published in Keyhole Crime.

KILLING WITH KINDNESS   *Anne Morice*

'Anne Morice has a gift for creating intelligent, affection generating characters set in bright and entertaining atmospheres' *Spectator*

STREETS OF DEATH   *Dell Shannon*

'Dell Shannon is now a great favourite on both sides of the Atlantic' *Financial Times*

A DANGEROUS FUNERAL   *Mary McMullen*

NOW READ ON WITH KEYHOLE CRIME
Other titles available in the shops now

MURDER AS USUAL   *Hugh Pentecost*

Mac Crenshaw, tipped as a future American president, is shot by a crazy woman who is herself bludgeoned to death seconds later. David Cotter arrives to investigate, but when his friend and assistant is murdered, David is determined to unmask the killer — at whatever cost.

THE MENACE WITHIN   *Ursula Curtiss*

When she is left in charge of her aunt's house, Amanda does not know of the secret underground shelter where a murderer is hidden. But the murderer knows about Amanda. And she has to be eliminated . . .

THE ROLLING HEADS
Aaron Marc Stein

When Matt Erridge stumbles across the breathtaking Barbie on the beach at Dinard, she soon persuades him to take her round Brittany. But if she hadn't been so set on going to Guimiliau, Matt might never have found her dead in the bushes.

 Keyhole Crime

A FEW CLUES ABOUT MORE GREAT TITLES YOU'LL SOON BE SEEING IN KEYHOLE CRIME

RANDOM KILLER *Hugh Pentecost*

Murder strikes the Beaumont one gentle spring day when the message comes through: 'There's a dead man in room 3406.' To his horror Pierre Chambrun, manager of New York's most luxurious hotel, discovers that a well-known TV interviewer has been strangled with picture wire.

First priority for Chambrun and his assistant Mark Haskell is to reassure the frightened guests. The second is to find the killer. But then the 'phone rings again: 'Picture wire job, room 1614. Same method, same result. Dead.'

WYCLIFFE AND THE SCAPEGOAT *W. J. Burley*

It is Hallowe'en and the Scapegoat in a grotesque mask and black cloak is tied inside the wheel of yew and laurel. The white robed man lights the leaves and amidst the roar of exploding fireworks the hoop of flame plunges into the sea.

Chief Superintendent Wycliffe enjoys the spectacle but when the undertaker Jonathan Riddle goes missing he finds himself directing a murder enquiry.

The locals believe the usually straw-filled Scapegoat was Riddle himself, but Wycliffe finds several different motives for the unpopular man's death.

 Keyhole Crime

ASK FOR ME TOMORROW
Margaret Millar

Wealthy, fifty-year-old Gilly Decker has lost one husband and is about to lose another. Gilly Decker's second husband, Marco, is a human vegetable who thirsts only for pills and the hypodermic needle. Why, then, does Gilly send bright young lawyer, Tom Aragon, to the wastes of Mexico to look for her first husband, B. J. Lockwood who, eight years ago, took off with one of the servants? Is she after B.J.'s money, B.J.'s son, or sweet revenge – and can she foresee the deadly future?

WELCOME TO THE GRAVE
Mary McMullen

Everything was going splendidly for Harley Ross. He was a highly successful novelist; he was rich and famous and he lived in a luxurious home in Connecticut with a beautiful mistress.

Then suddenly the impossible happened: Harley's estranged wife, Marta, returned and prepared to stay. He had to get her out – but Marta's weapon was Harley's guiltiest secret and it certainly entitled her to a meal-ticket for life. Or death.

Look out for them wherever you normally buy paperbacks

Keyhole Crime

If you have any difficulty obtaining any of these titles, or if you would like further information on forthcoming titles in Keyhole Crime please write to:-

Keyhole Crime, PO Box 236, Thornton Road, Croydon, Surrey CR9 3RU.